Books by
Mary Christner Borntrager

Ellie

Rebecca

Rachel

Daniel

Reuben

Andy

Polly

Sarah

Mandy

Over half a million books in print
in the Ellie's People Series.

This series is available
in regular type and
in large-print type.

Mandy

Mary Christner Borntrager

40148

HERALD PRESS
Scottdale, Pennsylvania
Waterloo, Ontario

Library of Congress Cataloging-in-Publication Data
Borntrager, Mary Christner, 1921-
    Mandy / Mary Christner Borntrager.
      p. cm. — (Ellie's people ; 9)
    ISBN 0-8361-9046-7 (alk. paper)
    I. Title. II. Series: Borntrager, Mary Christner, 1921- Ellie's
people ; 9.
    PS3552.O7544M36 1996
    813'.54—dc20   96-2461
                                              CIP

ISBN 0-8361-9046-7 (pbk.)
ISBN 0-8361-9048-3 (large-print pbk.)

The paper used in this publication is recycled and meets the minimum requirements of American National Standard for Information Sciences—Permanence of Paper for Printed Library Materials, ANSI Z39.48-1984.

Scripture is taken from the King James Version of *The Holy Bible,* with some adaptation to current English usage. This is a work of fiction but true to Amish life. The poem in chapter 22 is by the author.

MANDY
Copyright © 1996 by Herald Press, Scottdale, Pa. 15683
    Published simultaneously in Canada by Herald Press,
    Waterloo, Ont. N2L 6H7. All rights reserved
Library of Congress Catalog Number: 96-2461
International Standard Book Number: 0-8361-9048-3
Printed in the United States of America
Cover art by Edwin B. Wallace
Book design by Paula M. Johnson

05 04 03 02 01 00 99 98 97 96 10 9 8 7 6 5 4 3 2 1

To my sisters-in-law,
Ruth and Esther

ELLIE'S PEOPLE

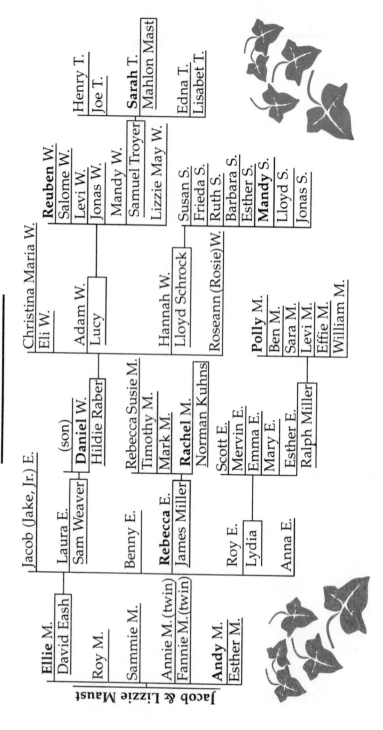

Contents

1
Six of a Kind

Mandy let the screen door slam behind her as she entered the house.

"*Sei net so laut* (don't be so loud)!" her sister Frieda scolded.

Then Frieda looked at seven-year-old Mandy and could plainly see that she was upset. "Did something happen at school today that made you so snappy?"

"Oh, that Lydia Yoder! She thinks she's so *schmaert* (smart)! All she does is brag. Just because I missed one spelling word, she made *Schpott* (fun) of me. I don't like her!"

"*Ach* (oh), she can only hurt you as much as you let her," Frieda answered her little sister. "Anyway, I think getting all words right except one is good."

"Not good enough for Lydia Yoder," Mandy replied.

"Well, anyway, go upstairs quietly and change into your chore clothes. I just baked a batch of sugar cookies, and when you come back, you may have one. Mom is taking a short nap, so go softly."

It seemed to Mandy that her mother took a lot of naps lately, but she didn't question her sister.

Her mother, Hannah, was a daughter of Daniel and Hildie Weaver. She was born two years after her Mother's return from a mysterious disappearance.

Mandy's Father was Lloyd Schrock. There were six girls in Lloyd and Hannah's family. Susan, the oldest, was nineteen. Frieda was seventeen, Ruth fourteen, Barbara thirteen, Esther eleven, and Mandy, the youngest, was seven.

Usually the four youngest girls walked home from their Amish one-room school together, but today was different. Ruth lagged behind to walk with her friend Leona. Barbara and Esther stayed to help Miss Zook sweep the floor, wash the chalkboard, and clean the erasers.

Mandy had been too upset to wait for them. Besides, sometimes Ruth and Leona talked about boys and didn't want her to hear. So this afternoon, she had run almost the entire mile from school. Mandy had even forgotten about old man Heffner's dog, who liked to bark at her.

Today, as she passed by on her way home from school, Boomer was nowhere in sight. Even if he had been, he would have had a hard time catching Mandy. Boomer was old and fat, just like his owner. Even their scowls seemed to look the same. Mr. Heffner was a bachelor who stayed mostly to himself.

When Mandy returned to the kitchen, her mother had finished her nap.

"Well, Mandy, *wo sin die Meed* (well, Mandy, where are the girls)?" her mother asked.

"Ach, they're coming. Ruth is with Leona, and Barbara and Esther stayed to help Teacher."

"You mean you walked home alone?"

"No, I ran. *Ich kann schteik schpringe* (I can run fast)!"

"Ach my, *ya* (yes), but I don't want you to go alone. From now on, you wait on the others."

"But Mom, Lydia Yoder made *Schpott* of me, and I didn't want to walk with the others."

"Don't you mind Lydia. Just stay with your sisters," her mother insisted.

"Here's the cookie I promised you." Frieda handed Mandy the treat. "Now don't eat it all in one bite." She laughed. Frieda's humor made Mandy feel better. Her sisters always knew how to brighten things up.

"Tonight after supper is all cleared away, I'll help you with your spelling words," Frieda offered.

That pleased Mandy. Tomorrow she would show that Lydia Yoder!

The other girls came trudging home, and then the evening activities began. Each helped the others, and work seemed lighter that way. Frieda stayed at the house and helped prepare the evening meal while Ruth, Barbara, and Esther went to the barn. Mandy gathered the eggs, fed the chickens, and filled the wood box. She often wished for a brother to relieve her of some of these tasks.

"Here come my three trusty helpers," Lloyd Schrock greeted his daughters as they prepared to do the milking.

"*Ya, doh sin mir* (yes, here we are)—Reuben, Ben, and Ezra," Ruth quipped.

"Aw, come on now," their dad protested. "You work just as well without boys' names."

True to her word, Frieda helped Mandy with her spelling, and in a trial test, she missed not a word. Now she was ready to face Lydia the next day.

Since it was Friday, Miss Zook asked the class if they would like a spelldown.

"Yes, let's!" agreed the children. "Boys against girls."

"All right, line up then," said Miss Zook. "Boys on the left, and girls on the right."

Lydia Yoder made sure she stood next to her friend Ada. Mandy heard her whisper, "I wish we didn't have Mandy on our side. She's sure to miss a word and cause our side to lose."

That made Mandy unsure of herself, and she missed the second word given to her. She went to her seat and bowed her head in shame.

Then she heard Lydia say, "She says her sisters helped her. Well, they are six of a kind. None of them must be very *schmaert*. My big brother helps me. He knows everything. Six of a kind, and she's the *Buppeli* (baby)."

2
Gut Buppelin

Mother had decided not go to church on Sunday. Mandy wondered about this, but she did not ask why. *Lately Mom has often missed church,* Mandy mused. *I wonder what's wrong?*

"Want to sit with me today at services?" Barbara asked Mandy as the girls straightened up the kitchen after breakfast.

"No, I sat with you two weeks ago. I think I'll sit with Susan today."

"Oh, that'll be nice," Susan responded. "Since I'm gone all week working as a *Maut* (hired girl) for Enos Beachys, we don't see much of each other."

"Ha!" laughed Frieda. "I wonder! If you sit where you can see Roman Troyer, you won't even know Mandy exists!"

"Stop that teasing!" Susan blushed. "You know Mandy *rutscht* (squirms) too much for me to forget her."

"I do not rutsch," Mandy declared.

"Then why did I have to keep nudging you last time?" Barbara reminded her.

"Well, maybe I did rutsche a little. But my knees were tired. My feet don't reach the floor, and the edge of the bench cuts into the back of my knees. You don't want my feet to go to sleep, do you?"

"I know the service seems long, but whenever you move, it makes the bench *gwiekt* (squeak)," Susan told her.

"I don't see why that bothers you, Susan," Barbara quipped. "That would only give Roman all the more reason to look your way."

Susan made a comical face and slapped at Barbara with her dish towel, all in fun, of course. The girls erupted into a fit of sisterly giggling.

For several months, Susan and Roman had been meeting at the Amish youth gatherings, such as singings, box socials, and corn huskings. Afterward, under cover of darkness, Roman would bring her home in his buggy.

Every other week, late on the Saturday night before a no-church Sunday, Roman would beam his flashlight on Susan's bedroom window. She would catch the signal and sneak downstairs quietly to visit with Roman or go for a walk with him.

Her sisters caught on to what was happening, and Susan endured a lot of teasing from them. But it was all good-natured fun.

Frieda started to say something more about Roman, but Susan quickly hushed her. "Frieda, if I were you, I wouldn't talk so much about Roman and me.

Jake's Samuel finds plenty of reasons to hang around and have a few words with you. Maybe something's going on."

Mandy saw her dad come to the kitchen door just as the girls finished cleaning up.

"Susan, come here," Dad called. "I want to talk with you alone. The rest of you girls go on upstairs and get ready for church. Susan will be up in a bit."

Frieda, Ruth, and Barbara looked knowingly at each other. Esther and Mandy were perplexed. Nevertheless, they made their way upstairs and began to dress for *die Gmee* (church).

Soon Susan climbed the stairs and came down the hall to the room where Mandy and Ruth were. Ruth was buttoning the back of Mandy's dress since she couldn't reach the buttons herself. As Susan entered the room, Mandy turned toward her.

"*Heb shtill* (hold still)," Ruth said with a sigh. "You are such a *Gwunnernaas* (wonder nose)."

"I'm not a Gwunnernaas," Mandy insisted. "I just want to know what Dad was talking about."

"He just told me he's not going along to church, and maybe I should stay home, too."

"But why?" Ruth exclaimed.

"*Now* who's a Gwunnernaas?" Mandy got back at her sister.

Ruth laughed. "You're right, Mandy. I guess I am a Gwunnernaas."

"Mom isn't feeling well," Susan explained, giving Ruth a wink.

"Oh, I know," Ruth answered knowingly, "but why both of you? Is something unusual? Or wrong?"

15

"No, Ruth. Dad just thinks Mom shouldn't be alone while he goes over to Coles to call."

"*Ya*, that's right."

Mandy had no idea what was going on, but she obediently finished dressing. As she tied her shoes, she remembered the seating plan for church. "Then who will I sit with, if Susan stays home?"

"Sit with me this time," Ruth offered. "I'll be your *Mamm* (mom) for today."

That pleased Mandy, and she ran downstairs and grabbed her coat.

"I've got Bess hitched up to the surrey, ready to go," Lloyd Schrock told his daughters. "Don't be in a hurry to come home. Drive carefully."

Mandy was glad to stay for lunch after the three-hour service in a neighbor's farmhouse. Being Amish, their congregation did not have a church building. The members took turns offering their homes for such occasions. They removed partitions downstairs to make a large room.

A closed-in wagon called the *Bankwagge* (bench wagon) delivered the backless benches for seating. After preaching, a meal and fellowship time were enjoyed by the whole gathering.

For the meal, some benches were pushed together in pairs, with longer legs folded down to make tables. Other benches were the seats. Since there were so many, they ate in stages, with groups coming in turn to the tables.

"Let's play with the babies while their mothers eat," Mandy's friend Alma suggested.

"All right, let's do that," Mandy agreed. "But I hope

16

I don't get a cry *Buppeli* (baby). Last time I tried to take Fannie Bontrager's *Buppeli*. I guess he was afraid of me, because he yelled so loud.

"His mom asked if I pinched him. Of course I didn't! But I almost felt like it. Then at least I would have known why he yelled."

"Oh, Mandy, you wouldn't!" Alma exclaimed.

"No, I'd never do such a thing. But this time I'm going to pick a girl baby. I don't think they cry so loud."

The girls found some weary mothers willing to share their babies. They cuddled the babies until Mandy's sister Frieda told her it was time to go home. "We've got to get back for the milking. The cows are waiting for us, and maybe somebody else is too."

"I've got to go now, Alma," she told her friend. "Maybe next church Sunday we can take care of babies again."

"I hope so," Alma answered. "Today we had *gut Buppelin* (good babies). Let's pick the same ones next time."

With that plan in mind, the two girls said their good-byes.

3

A Brother at Last

All the way home, the older girls kept whispering. Mandy couldn't hear what they were saying, but they seemed to be excited about something.

"Why do you whisper so? Are you talking about me?" Mandy asked.

"No, we aren't talking about you," Ruth assured her.

"Well, then, talk loud enough so I can hear. I want to know what you're saying," Mandy demanded.

"You'll find out soon enough," Frieda told her.

"Why not now?" she grumbled.

"Just be patient," Esther advised her.

In fact Esther, only eleven, was not sure why her sisters were so secretive either.

"Bet they're talking about *Buwe* (boys) again," she told Mandy.

"*Ya*, Buwe, Buwe, that's all they think of," Mandy remarked. "I think boys are yucky. Except maybe little boy babies, and even they cry more than girl babies do."

Barbara laughed. "How do you know that?"

"Because Alma and I have taken care of lots of babies after church, and the Buwe yell and cry so loud."

"You had a pretty good set of lungs and cried loud enough yourself, as I remember when you were a baby, Mandy," Barbara said.

"*Ich hab net* (I did not)!" Mandy exclaimed.

The conversation ceased as a car approached, sending up spirals of dust. Bess shied, and Frieda worked hard to control her. For one frightening moment the girls thought the buggy would upset. They clung to each other for protection.

The car passed, spraying small gravel stones as it rattled on down the road. Bess ran faster than ever, causing the buggy to sway back and forth.

"*Ach, mei Hatz* (oh, my heart)!" Esther exclaimed. "Will we upset?"

"No," Frieda answered. "Just hold on. I'll get Bess under control." She did, too, by firmly speaking to her. "Whoa, Bess, whoa," she gentled the mare.

"That was Dr. Gray," Ruth observed after things quieted down.

"*Ya*, he waved and blew his horn. I think that loud noise from the horn is what made Bess act up."

"Maybe so," Barbara answered.

"He was headed back toward town, and we know what that means," Frieda remarked, smiling knowingly.

"He was going home from church, too," Mandy guessed. "Where is his church, anyway?"

"Oh, I doubt that he was going home from church. He probably made a house call," Ruth responded.

"But who would need a doctor out our way today?" Mandy questioned. "Everyone was in church." Then she thought of something and was frightened. "Everyone except Mom, Dad, and Susan. Oh, Mom was not feeling well. Do you think she is bad off?"

"No, Mandy," Frieda assured her sister. "If it was Mom the doctor came to see, he knew what to do."

The girls looked at each other and smiled. *How can they be so sure?* Mandy wondered.

As the buggy turned in the driveway of the Schrock home, Daddy Lloyd came out to meet his daughters. He was smiling broadly.

"Any news, Dad?" Barbara asked.

"*Ya,*" their Father said, grinning more than ever. He began to unhitch the horse.

"Don't keep us waiting!" Frieda burst out.

"You are no longer six of a kind. We are seven now, and one is a boy."

"Is everything all right?" Barbara asked.

"Seems to be," Dad answered.

The girls were already halfway across the yard. Mandy still didn't understand, but she hurried after the others.

"What's wrong, Ruth?" she asked as she ran to catch up.

"*Mir hawwe en nei Buppeli* (we have a new baby), and it's a boy," Ruth explained.

Mandy's feet took wings. Did she understand what Ruth said? Was it really true?

Susan met her siblings in the kitchen.

"Susan," Mandy gasped, all out of breath. "Susan, *is es waahr* (is it true)? Do we really have a Buppeli?"

"Yes, Mandy, it's true."

"And is it a boy baby?"

"Yes, it's a boy. Come, I'll show you." Susan led Mandy to her parents' bedroom, where her sisters were already oohing and ahing over a tiny bundle.

"Oh, look at that head of black hair!" Barbara exclaimed.

"Such little hands," Esther remarked.

"Let me see," demanded Mandy. "Oh, is he ours to keep?"

"Of course," Mother answered. "I wouldn't give him away for anything."

"May I hold him?" Mandy begged.

"Not yet, Mandy," Susan said. "He's just newborn. We'll let him rest awhile. You'll get a chance later."

"You'll have to share him with five others," Dad instructed. The girls had been so engrossed in admiring their new brother that they had not heard their father come in.

"I don't care if I have to share," Mandy declared. "I'm just glad I have a brother—at last." Then she added, "Even if boy babies cry more and yell louder."

4
So There, Lydia!

Chore time could not pass quickly enough for Mandy. Mom had promised that she could hold her baby brother after the chores. In her haste she spilled a lot of chicken feed and while gathering eggs broke a few. Then, rushing to the house with the last armful of firewood, she stumbled and dropped it all on the kitchen floor.

"Don't be so *doppich* (careless)," Susan scolded. "What's your hurry?"

"Mom promised that I could hold the baby after I do my chores," Mandy told her.

"Well now, just for hurrying so, you must clean up this mess," Susan insisted.

"But Mom said after my chores, and this is after," Mandy complained. "If I wait, then someone else will get him first."

"Don't worry. He'll keep, and you'll get your turn." Susan handed Mandy the broom and dustpan. "Sweep up. Your chores aren't finished until you clean up after yourself. Then wash your hands real good and put on a clean apron. And be sure your hands are nice and warm before you go to the bedroom."

Mandy took the broom and made short work of cleaning up. Then she washed her hands and went upstairs to change to a clean apron. She was eager to get finished before her sisters completed their work!

Frieda, Ruth, and Barbara were the barn helpers. Esther carried water for cooking and various uses. She also kept the kerosene lamps filled and their chimneys clean. Then there were the calves to feed. Sometimes they could be so difficult. If they were extra greedy, they would butt the pail and spill the milk.

Esther was also eager to finish her tasks, but she could not make Spotty the calf behave, so she was late coming to the house. As she entered the kitchen, she heard Mandy say, "I'm ready, Susan."

"Come quietly, then," Susan responded. "Mom is resting. Pull up the rocker closer to the bed."

"What was that racket in the kitchen a while ago?" Mother asked. "It sounded like wood falling. It did *schreck mich wunderbaar* (scare me terribly)."

"That's exactly what it was," Susan confirmed. "Mandy was *schusslich* (careless) and dropped an armful. She just couldn't wait to get in here to cuddle the baby."

"You will have plenty of chances to hold him," Mother assured her. "You will be *my Kindsmaut* (babysitter)."

That pleased Mandy. She would never get tired of caring for the *Buppeli*. Mandy reached into the wooden cradle, ready to pick up her precious baby brother.

"No, no," Susan stopped her. "You sit in the rocker, and I'll give him to you."

"He's so little!" Mandy exclaimed as she took him in her arms. "Look at his little fingers! Are his toes so tiny too?"

"Well, let's see." Susan unfolded the soft blue blanket.

"Really!" Mandy marveled. "They're so pink and cute. Wait till I tell that Lydia Yoder at school tomorrow that we have a *schnuck Buppeli* (cute baby). She thinks no one has a schnucker baby than her baby sister. Well, I'll tell her different."

"*Ach*, Mandy," Hannah told her daughter, "all babies are schnuck. We must not be proud. Let's just thank God for giving him to us."

Mandy said no more about Lydia Yoder, but in her heart she determined to do exactly as planned.

Esther came into the room and begged for her turn to rock the baby.

"But I didn't have him very long," Mandy objected.

"You had him long enough." Susan took the bundle and handed him to Esther.

"Mom, why does the baby stick his tongue out?" Mandy asked. "I thought it was bad to do that."

"All little babies stick their tongues out sometimes. Maybe he's getting hungry," Susan answered. She had noticed, too, that his tongue seemed larger than normal and seemed to protrude from his lips.

Then Susan gave directions to the others. "Esther, I'll let you hold him five minutes yet, then you come and help get supper. Mandy, start setting the table.

You need not set a place for Mom. We'll fix a tray and take it to her."

"May I bring her the tray?" Mandy asked.

"No," stated Susan, "one of us older girls will carry it in."

Mandy was disappointed. She wanted a chance to look at the baby again.

"Dad," Frieda asked as they sat around the table, "what are we going to name the baby? We can't just call him Buppeli."

"Mom wants to name him Lloyd." Dad beamed his pleasure. "She says it's to carry on the family name. So that's settled."

"But there'll be two Lloyds in our family," Mandy objected.

"You'll call me Dad and my son, Lloyd, so it won't be confusing."

Mandy was so excited when she started to school on Monday morning. The first thing she did was catch up to Lydia Yoder.

"We have a boy baby, and his name is Lloyd. He's schnucker than your baby sister. So there, Lydia!"

Mandy had actually said it.

5
It Can't Be True

Mandy came home from school with a happy, satisfied feeling. For once she had put Lydia Yoder in her place. Setting her lunch pail on the kitchen table, she hurried to the bedroom.

"May I hold the baby before I start my chores?" she asked.

"No, Mandy," Frieda answered. "He's just fallen asleep."

Thinking her mother might give her consent, she turned to her. "May I, Mom, just *glee bissel* (a little bit)?"

"Not now," Mother replied. Her voice sounded strange. Mandy looked at her and saw she was crying. Hannah Schrock blew her nose into the large white hankie she kept nearby.

"Mom, *was is letz* (what's wrong)?" Mandy was frightened. Never had she seen her mother cry except at funerals.

"Come," Frieda invited her. "Let's go to the kitchen, and I'll tell you. Mom doesn't feel like talking right now."

"She's crying," Mandy observed. "The only time I ever see her cry is at funerals. Did someone die?"

"Nobody died, Mandy."

"Well then, what is it?"

Barbara, Ruth, and Esther came into the kitchen at the same time.

"Mandy, you should wait on us. It's not safe for you to run ahead," Ruth said.

"Mom's crying," Mandy informed them.

"What! Why is she crying?" Barbara quizzed Frieda.

Without waiting for an answer, the girls started for the bedroom.

However, Frieda stepped in front of them. "I think it might be better if you don't go in there for now. I believe Mom would rather be alone for a while."

"But why?" Esther asked. "What happened?"

"She had a hard day trying to feed the baby. He couldn't seem to nurse right. Dad will tell you tonight what the doctor had to say. He came today and explained things."

"What things?" Ruth asked.

"He didn't talk with me. Dad can tell you. Look what time it is. The clock keeps ticking away as we stand here talking. Let's get to the chores."

Mandy didn't even care for a half-moon pie or a piece of homemade apple butter bread, her usual after-school snack. She just stood in bewilderment until Frieda urged her, "*Mach schnell* (hurry up)!"

27

Somberly the girls went about their duties. Dad was not his cheerful self when the girls joined him at the barn. Mechanically each one did their work. When they returned to the house, Frieda had supper ready: a steaming kettle of cooked cornmeal mush, baked potatoes, ham, gravy, green beans, and half-moon pies.

Susan, the oldest of the girls, had left that morning for her *Maut* (hired girl) job at Enos Beachy's. The rest of the family prepared for their evening meal.

Frieda was a good organizer. "Fill the water glasses, Mandy. And Ruth, slice the bread. Esther, get a pitcher of milk for our mush. Barbara, get the potatoes out of the oven. I'll fix a tray for Mom."

Lloyd Schrock had gone to talk with his wife after he had washed up.

"May I carry Mom's tray in this time?" Mandy begged.

"If you're very careful and come right back, I'll let you," Frieda agreed.

However, Mandy was met at the door by her dad. "Mom says she doesn't want to eat." He took the tray. "Mandy, you go on out to the kitchen. Tell the girls I'll be there in a little bit."

Why is everyone so quiet? Mandy did not like it! As Father sat down to the table, she detected a tear slowly trickling down his cheek. With his toil-worn hand, he brushed it away. All heads bowed in silent prayer as each one's thoughts ascended heavenward.

"Dad, tell us what's wrong," Mandy demanded.

"You girls have a right to know, and I suppose this is as good a time as any. Frieda is already aware of the problem. We have a mongoloid baby." Dad's voice broke, and he covered his face with his hands.

"What does that mean?" Mandy asked.

After clearing his throat, Dad continued. "It means he is different from most children. The doctor told us this afternoon. We should have noticed it by the low-set ears and his slightly enlarged tongue. The back of his head is rather flat, but many babies' heads are odd-shaped at birth. I guess we were so pleased to finally have a son that Mom and I never noticed."

"Oh, it can't be true!" Barbara gasped.

No one felt like eating. After supper Barbara asked, "Dad, will his mind be all right?" She had to know. Everyone stopped clearing the table to hear the answer.

"No, Barbara, the doctor says we must prepare for a mentally handicapped boy. But God has given him to us to love and care for, and that's what we'll do."

Lloyd went to comfort his wife. Mandy saw him take the prayer book and knew he and Mother would pray.

"I'll pray, too," she murmured to herself. "Lloyd is still the prettiest baby in the world."

6

The Stone Quarry

Many women from the church came to visit Hannah Schrock and her new baby. Among them was Anna Yoder and her daughter, Lydia. Frieda invited them to come in.

It was Saturday, so all the scholars were home and busy around the house. Every room had to be cleaned, the lamp chimneys washed and shined, both stoves polished, baking attended to, and many other things done. Today they were going to dig the late potatoes and store them in the bin.

"We came to see your new *Buppeli*," Lydia informed Mandy, smiling pleasantly.

"He's in de *Bettschtubb* (bedroom)," Mandy said. She thought, *My, my, Lydia is all peaches and cream now. If Ada were here, Lydia wouldn't be so friendly to me.* Putting her feelings aside, she invited Lydia to follow her.

Anna Yoder shook hands with Hannah. "How are you getting along?"

"Oh, I'm doing alright, and we have a *gut* (good) baby. He sleeps a lot more than my girls did and sure doesn't cry as much. They were all colicky."

Lydia and Mandy went straight to the cradle.

"He sure has a lot of hair!" Lydia exclaimed. "But he looks different, not like most Amish babies."

"*Ach*, Lydia," Anna chided her daughter. "Of course he's an Amish Buppeli. He belongs to Lloyd and Hannah." Then Anna looked at the sleeping bundle and understood why Lydia made such a remark. The child had distinctly different features. As Anna resumed her visit with Hannah, Mandy noticed that her eyes had softened with pity.

"You girls go on out now. We want to visit with each other," Hannah told Mandy. "You must get your regular Saturday work done and then help Barbara and Esther dig potatoes."

"Do you always have so much work to do?" Lydia asked.

"*Ya*, there's always something," Mandy assured her.

"Well, at my house, we have boys dig the potatoes. I get to play on Saturday afternoon," Lydia bragged.

There she goes again, Mandy thought. *Brag, brag, brag!* Just once she wished she could find something bigger or better than this girl had. *That would be wunderbaar (wonderful)!* she told herself.

The girls went out to the rope swing. Barbara had told Mandy she would let them play for twenty minutes. After that, Mandy had to help pick up potatoes.

"Push me first," Lydia demanded.

Mandy pushed her as high as she could. Lydia

yelled as though she was scared. But when Mandy tried to stop her, she called out, "No, higher, higher!"

Mandy's arms were getting tired, and finally she declared, "My turn, Lydia."

"Who said we're taking turns?" Lydia hopped off the swing and started across the lawn. "Let's wade in the ditch by your garden. I like to *suddle* (splash) in water."

"Ach my, no! We aren't allowed to," Mandy told her.

"My mom *gebt nix drum* (doesn't care)," Lydia retorted, running toward the stream that flowed by the garden.

"Mandy," Barbara called. "Come now. It's time to get to the truck patch and start work on the *Grumm-beere* (potatoes)."

Mandy was glad her sister called her. Lydia was about to wade in the water, but now she turned and followed the girls. Reluctantly she picked up a few potatoes as Barbara unearthed them.

"Look at the funny one I found," Esther laughed. "It looks like a little old man."

"Here is an odd one, too." Mandy displayed a misshapen brown glob. There were several small potatoes clinging to a strangely formed larger one.

"That looks just like a pig," giggled Esther.

"Let's see who can find the biggest one," Barbara suggested. She was trying to make the job seem more like fun.

Several times Lydia called out, "Here's a big one. I found the biggest," but they were only brown stones. The girls laughed good-naturedly at her mistake. They knew from experience how easy it was to take a stone for a potato before the dirt was brushed off.

But after a while, Lydia began to complain. "This is nothing but a stone quarry. I didn't come here to work. I came to see the baby. Now I'm going to the house, and maybe Mom will let me hold the baby before we go home."

Mandy was glad to see her go. It wasn't fun to have her around when she grumbled so.

Just before the Yoder visitors left, the Schrock sisters brought the first wheelbarrow of potatoes to the house.

"Well, girls, it looks like you have a good crop this year," Anna Yoder complimented them. "You're good workers, and your mother needs your *Hilf* (help) now more than ever."

"Ya," Lydia said, "I helped in the stone quarry, too."

Her mother did not understand that remark, but later she found out what her daughter meant.

Mandy sure was glad when they left.

7

One True Friend

That first Sunday at church with her baby brother was not at all the way Mandy had pictured it. No, not at all!

Baby Lloyd was now almost five weeks old. It seemed strange for the older girls to see Mother holding the small bundle on her lap again. It had been seven years since Mandy was born. Since Mandy had been the youngest until Lloyd was born, she had never seen her mom caring for a younger brother or sister.

"Mom, may I take care of the baby while you eat after church?" Mandy asked.

"Oh, I expect there'll be plenty of others willing to help," Mother answered. "Perhaps he'll be sleeping at that time. You know he does sleep a lot."

"But if he isn't sleeping, then may I have him?" begged Mandy.

"You heard your mother," Lloyd told his daughter. "There'll be plenty of chances for you to take care of him at home. Let the older girls help Mom this time."

Mandy did not reply. She knew Dad's word was the final say. Besides, she just knew sometime she would get to show him off at church.

Most of the way to church was traveled in silence. No doubt Hannah and Lloyd were dreading the pity others would bestow upon them. They did not need or want pity. All they asked for was encouragement and support from their fellow brothers and sisters in the church.

Mandy was glad when they finally arrived at the Stoltzfus home, where services were held that Sunday.

As they climbed out of the buggy, Mandy said, *"Heit hock ich bei der* (today I sit with you), right, Mom?"

"Ya, today you sit with me," her mother assured her. "Bring along the *Windelsackli* (diaper bag)."

At least if she couldn't carry the baby to the house, Mandy thought, she could follow closely with the Windelsackli.

Only Esther and Mandy had come along with their parents in the surrey. The other girls were driving the open buggy. Esther had just begun to wear a cape dress and was allowed to sit with her friends.

"Let me take your baby," Edna Kaufman offered as soon as Hannah stepped inside the door, "at least until you've laid aside your shawl and bonnet."

"Danki (thanks), Edna." Hannah handed the sleeping child to her.

"Oh, my, he sure has a head full of hair!" Edna exclaimed. "I don't recall any of your girls with such a lot of hair, and he doesn't favor any of them, does he?"

"No, he doesn't," Hannah answered, almost as though defending her son.

Edna caught the tone of her voice and sincerely remarked, "He is a pretty child."

Hannah didn't answer except to say, "*Ya*, well. Come, Mandy, we'll go in now." Taking her baby, she and Mandy found a space on one of the backless benches in the kitchen. Many eyes turned toward them as they entered. It was hard for Mandy to hide her pride, but her mom was struggling to prepare her mind for worship.

To Mandy the service seemed endless. She had a hard time not to *rutsche* (squirm). Baby Lloyd slept most of the time, except when Hannah took him to a small side room to nurse him. He was still slow at that, and Mandy did a lot of rutsching while Mother was out of the room.

Finally the last song reminded her that church was almost over and she could join the other young girls. They would probably all want to see her new baby brother.

"Want to see our new baby?" she asked right away as she joined Lydia, Katie, Fannie, Sara, and Alma.

"I've already seen him," Lydia told the others. "But let's go anyway. He's different. Come on, I'll show you." Lydia was a leader, and other girls let her lead them, sometimes into trouble.

The girls made their way to the bedroom where several infants lay sleeping.

"Here he is," Mandy whispered, pleased to let the girls look at baby Lloyd.

"*Ya, datt is er mit die Zung aus* (yes, there he is with

his tongue out)," laughed Lydia, "just like a sleeping dog."

Mandy looked at her in amazement. She felt like slapping her. This was her precious little brother, and Lydia was making fun of him.

"I think he is *schnuck* (cute)," Alma declared.

"Oh, well, you would," Lydia sputtered. "You wouldn't know a cute baby if you saw one. Come on, girls, let's go. I heard my mother tell my dad that the Schrocks have a retarded baby. That's nothing to be proud of."

All the girls turned and followed Lydia except one. "Don't pay any attention to her," soothed Alma. "The only way she knows to get attention is by being mean. I don't see why the girls follow her."

"What does *retarded* mean?" Mandy asked.

"I think it means when they don't understand things very well. But then, everybody's different. Don't let what Lydia said worry you. I'm your friend and will always be. You are a nice girl, and you have a beautiful brother."

"Let's always be friends, Alma," Mandy answered. "When I have a true friend like you, Lydia doesn't matter. As long as I have one true friend, I'll be happy. One true friend is better than a dozen like Lydia."

Alma agreed.

8

Was It Nellie?

"May I stay up and take care of the baby?" Mandy asked one night.

Mother and the older girls had taken turns caring for baby Lloyd when he could not rest. That meant many sleepless nights were spent in the Schrock home.

"*Ach*, Mandy, *du bist so yung* (you're so young)," Mother replied. "Do you really think you could?"

"*Ya*, I'm sure! And tomorrow is Saturday, so I don't need to get up in time for school."

"Oh, so you figured that out, did you?" her sister Ruth remarked. "Along about one o'clock in the morning, you'll get pretty sleepy."

"Please let me," Mandy begged her mother. She just loved to rock her little brother in the comfortable hickory rocker.

Baby Lloyd seemed to be getting his days and nights mixed up. Usually he slept well most of the day except at feeding time. Even then Mother had to wake him occasionally.

"Finish your chores once, and let me think about it. I'll see what Dad says," Hannah told her daughter.

Mandy knew that Mother never made important decisions without first consulting Father. How she was wishing that this time he would say yes!

"Have you asked him?" was Mandy's first question as she came in from finishing her outdoor work.

"Ach my, no, Mandy. You're too *ungeduldich* (impatient). Dad has not come in from the barn yet. Now wash up, and set the table, and don't ask me again."

Mandy did as she was told, but it wasn't easy for her. Several times she bit her lip to keep from asking again. When her father walked into the kitchen, she was trying so hard to overhear her parents' talking with each other that she dropped a plate. It broke into many pieces.

"See, Mandy," Barbara chided, "if you can't hold onto a plate, you might drop the baby, too."

"Oh, I wouldn't," declared Mandy. "Really, I wouldn't. The plate just slipped. I'll *butz* (clean) it up right away."

All during supper, the family kept up a pleasant conversation. But not once was it mentioned who would take care of the baby that night. And Mandy did not dare ask, since she had been warned.

During the time she and Ruth were doing dishes, Mandy did say, "*Was denkst du* (what do you think)?"

"What do you mean, what do I think'?" Ruth responded. She knew what Mandy meant and just wanted to string her along for a bit.

"Do you think they'll let me take care of the baby during the night?" Mandy asked.

"That's up to Mom and Dad to decide. But if it were my choice I'd say *net* (not). You are way too *schusslich* (careless)," Ruth declared.

"*Ich bin net schusslich* (I am not careless), and if Mom says yes, I'll prove I'm not."

"Well, she hasn't said anything yet," her sister reminded her.

Mandy wished her mother would at least say *something*. Not knowing was almost harder to take than if she said *net*.

Once the dishes were done and the kitchen cleaned up, Mandy joined her parents in the living room. She sat quietly by Mother's rocker and watched her mend a pair of socks. Every once in a while, she glanced over at her dad, reading the *Farm Journal*.

Neither one seemed to notice her, or so Mandy thought. Finally she *rutsched* (squirmed) and cleared her throat. Mother looked at her and smiled. She would not keep her waiting any longer.

"Lloyd," she addressed her husband, "Mandy wants to stay up tonight and tend the baby, if he needs tending. What do you think about that?"

Lloyd lowered the magazine, peered out over his glasses, and just looked at Mandy. Finally he spoke. "Isn't she too young for a responsibility like that? But it's up to you."

"I am willing to let her try," Hannah stated. "She helps take care of him during the day and does real well."

It was settled. Mandy felt relieved and quite

grown-up. *Just wait until Sunday, and I can tell Alma and Lydia!*

Mandy had made a floor bed with a blanket and pillow close to the heating stove. Sure enough, at eleven-thirty she heard the baby begin to fuss. Quickly she put the bottle of milk in the teakettle on top of the stove, so it would warm up. After changing baby Lloyd, she sat down in the rocker to feed him.

The house was so quiet. Never had the mantle clock ticked so loudly. Suddenly a loud, eerie howl broke the silence. At first Mandy's blood seemed to freeze. As the second howl sounded, she shot up like a flash and ran with the baby in her arms. She jumped right up on the bed.

"*Was is der* (what's with you)?" Dad asked as he sat bolt upright.

"A wolf!" exclaimed Mandy, trembling.

"Ach, it was only our dog, Nellie," Mother assured her, taking the baby. "Thanks for your help. Now go on up to bed. I'll take care of him the rest of the night."

Still shaking, Mandy made her way upstairs and pulled her covers over her ears, asking herself, *Was it really Nellie?*

9

A Haughty Spirit

Mandy went to bed as she had been told, but sleep eluded her. The sound of that bloodcurdling howl had unnerved her greatly. It seemed to come from right outside the door.

However, Mandy knew Mother did not allow their good dog Nellie on the porch because she tracked mud. Many times the girls or Mother chased her away with a broom or mop, whatever they happened to have in hand. By now, the dog was well trained to stay off the porch.

Morning finally came. Mandy heard her father shaking the stove grate to sift the ashes. She knew he soon would call them to come downstairs and start chores. But Mandy wasn't ready to get up. She thought she had hardly slept all night and was fighting a headache.

Sure enough, Lloyd Schrock called up the stairs, *"Meed, es is Zeit uff schteh* (girls, it's time to get up)."

"*Ach*, do I have to?" Mandy mumbled sleepily to Esther, with whom she shared a bed.

"Not this morning, since you were up late last night with Lloydie," Esther told her. "You can sleep some more, and we'll do your chores for you this time. Then we'll call you for breakfast when we get back to the house."

Mandy thanked Esther and rolled over for another snooze while the older sisters helped their father in the barn. Esther gathered the eggs that morning.

After breakfast, the girls were washing the dishes and putting them away. Mandy was still tired and moping around, barely doing her share of the work.

"Why are you so grumpy, anyway?" Barbara asked Mandy. "I suppose staying up with the baby at night isn't so much fun after all, is it?"

"Taking care of the baby was all right, but Nellie howled so loud it scared me."

"So that's why you came upstairs and were trembling. I heard you, but when you climbed into bed and pulled the covers over your head, I thought I'd just let you go to sleep." Esther chuckled.

"Don't laugh! You would have been frightened, too," Mandy protested.

"Why, what makes you think so? We've often heard old Nellie half bark, half howl."

"But never in the still of night. And if it was Nellie, she didn't even bark this time. She just howled like a wolf."

"Well, anyway, we'd better forget about that. Let the wild be wild."

Mother came into the kitchen after putting Lloydie

back to bed. "What took you girls so long cleaning up?"

"Ach, Mandy was telling me about what happened during the night," Esther said.

"Mandy," Mom told her, "I'm glad you wanted to help care for Lloydie, but don't ever again run like you did with the baby in your arms. Why, you could have dropped him. *Es hot mich wunderbaar verschrocke* (it scared me terribly)!"

"What happened?" Esther asked.

"We'll forget it now," Mother replied. "*Mach schnell* (hurry up) now, and get to your Saturday cleaning. Tomorrow is our *Gmee Sunndaag* (church Sunday), and we want to be ready to leave early for church."

If it were the in-between Sunday, when they had no church, they could be more relaxed because they would likely be staying home.

"We don't want to be late for church," Mom added. She wished that just once they could get to church before Lewis Krofts. Lewis Kate (Lewis's wife) always had such a smug look and made remarks about folks who liked to lie in bed on Sunday mornings.

But I must not have such thoughts, Hannah mused. *I must not judge another.*

Mandy had looked forward to this Sunday and the chance to tell Alma, Lydia, and other girls how she took care of her brother on Friday night. Now that her bubble had burst, she almost dreaded going to church.

One bright spot remained. She could see her friend, Alma. They told each other their secrets and knew only they would know them. It was so good to have someone to trust. She could even tell Alma about

44

her frightening experience during the night. Alma wouldn't laugh at her.

That night Mandy went to bed early so she could catch up on her sleep and be ready for doing her chores quickly on Sunday morning. Finally the work was done up, breakfast was over with, and the family was on their way. They had to take two buggies, and the older girls had already left.

"Bring the *Windelsackli* (diaper bag), Mandy, and *mach schnell*," Mother said as she headed down the porch steps. "I suppose Lewis Krofts are there already," she added without thinking as she handed her husband the baby and climbed into the surrey.

"What does that matter?" Lloyd asked. "We don't go to suit Lewis Kate. I hope we go to worship. Let's remain humble."

Hannah certainly felt rebuked by her husband's response to what slipped out of her mouth. But she knew he was right.

The bishop's sermon was taken from Proverbs sixteen, verse eighteen: "Pride goes before destruction, and a haughty spirit before a fall." Hannah felt smitten by her former attitude, and in her heart she was making her peace with God. The bishop preached so plainly that even the young children understood.

"I shall leave the German for a bit and speak in the tongue that we use in our homes, so *die kleine Kinder* (the little children) can understand better," he announced at one point.

Mandy listened and felt uneasy about her plans for boasting to Lydia.

The bishop preached in a singsong manner which

began to make Mandy drowsy. Suddenly there was a bump, and Mandy found herself on the floor. She had dozed off for just a second. Quickly she got up. Sitting next to her mother, she tried to hide her face against her shoulder.

Some of the women smiled. Mandy was glad when they went home after the meal and fellowship. She felt she must tell her mother something.

"Oh, Mom, I was going to brag to Lydia and be proud. But it's like the bishop said. I fell—in front of all those people. I'm so ashamed of what I planned to do."

"I know how you feel," her mother consoled her. "I had to make some peace, too. We both learned a lesson today."

10
Mumbling Mandy

Time passed, and baby Lloyd was no longer a baby. Although he was now five years old, he still took a lot of care. He had taken a special liking to Mandy, and she was responsible for much of his care.

Only recently had little Lloyd learned to walk. It was more of a shuffle, and he followed Mandy everywhere. He was quite affectionate and usually smiling that crooked little grin.

Lloydie could not talk but made certain sounds for certain needs. If he wanted a drink of water, he made sipping noises. When hungry, he acted as if he were chewing. If Mandy was out of his sight, he might call "Dee-Dee" until she returned.

When little Lloyd was born, Mandy had been so excited. What fun it would be taking care of a baby! But now Lloyd was no longer a baby, and he took up so much of her time.

Mandy was now in the sixth grade. One day she

came home from school and tried to sneak in unnoticed. Little Lloyd caught sight of her as she passed by the living room. Immediately he shuffled to the kitchen, calling "Dee-Dee."

"*Ach* (oh), you little *Badder* (bother)," Mandy complained. "Can't I even have time to put my lunch pail away? All I want is a half-moon pie before I do my work. Now I suppose I'll have to feed you, too."

Lloyd just looked at his sister and grinned happily.

"Mandy," Mother called, "before you gather the eggs, I want you to finish bringing the clothes in from the line. Take your brother with you."

"Ach, Mom, I can go faster without him," Mandy protested.

"*Es macht nix aus* (that doesn't matter). He hasn't been outdoors all day. Now *mach schnell* (hurry)."

There is no way I can mach schnell with little Lloyd along, Mandy thought. She quickly ate her half-moon pie, giving enough to her brother to keep him quiet. One could not savor the delicious taste by eating so fast, and Mandy resented that.

She took the laundry basket in one hand and led her brother with the other as she headed for the clothesline. All her sisters were busy with various tasks.

The older girls were helping their father put up the last cutting of hay. Mother and Barbara had been shelling lima beans and canning them. In the afternoon some out-of-state company unexpectedly stopped by for an hour's visit. It had been a busy day. They hadn't had time yet to bring in the laundry and dampen it for ironing the next day.

Mandy could hardly reach the clothespins to un-fasten the different articles. She did like the nice out-door, fresh smell of each garment. Mother knew how to get their white things dazzling.

Mandy worked with her eyes and mind on the job at hand until she heard her brother giggling. Turning around, she gasped. Most of the clothes Mandy had placed in the basket were on the grass, and little Lloyd was walking all over them.

"Ach, Lloydie, *du bist nixnutzich* (you're naughty). How am I supposed to get anything done with you around?"

As she reached for him, he fell onto a sheet, wrap-ping himself into it and rolling on the ground.

Mandy had had enough. She undid the sheet and half-dragged him to the inside yard. Closing the gate, she remarked, "You can call all you want to. I can't do my work with you around."

Ruth heard her brother yelling and crying. She came to his rescue. This did not satisfy little Lloyd. He was much happier outside with Mandy, playing in the clean laundry.

"Mandy," Mother asked her daughter as she car-ried the basket indoors, "why did you shut your broth-er in the yard? Didn't I tell you to take him along with you?"

"*Ya*, Mom, but he threw the clean clothes out on the ground and walked all over them. He wrapped himself up in one of the sheets, and I could hardly get him untangled. It's too hard to work and take care of him, too."

"Maybe I expect too much from you," her mother

pondered. "It seems when you're around, he wants only you. He really does enjoy being with you. Try to understand that he's not like other children. We must be patient with him."

Mother didn't need to remind Mandy that her little brother was different. Lydia and her group did that often enough. By now, Mandy almost dreaded going to church anymore. The snide remarks other young folks made really hurt.

Lloydie tagged along as Mandy went to gather the eggs. On their way back to the house, he ran right in front of her. She stumbled, dropping the basket of eggs, and breaking many of them. *Now what will Mother say?* Mandy wondered.

As Mandy set the remaining eggs on the pantry shelf, she muttered quietly to herself. "He always causes trouble, and I have to be patient."

"What are you mumbling about?" her sister Esther asked.

"Ach, *nix* (nothing)," Mandy answered.

"Well, then, I guess we will call you mumbling Mandy," she laughed.

"So, go ahead!" retorted Mandy.

11
A Schnepper Box

Mandy sat up straight and listened carefully. It was their church Sunday. Although she didn't understand much of the sermon, she always got the last part. That was when the bishop announced upcoming weddings and the place for the next Sunday services.

"If it is the Lord's will, we shall gather at Lloyd Schrock's in two weeks," the bishop stated.

Mandy shivered with excitement. She loved it when church services were held at their home.

"*Hock shtill* (sit still)!" her mother warned her in a whisper.

Mandy tried but, oh, it was so hard, at the end of a morning of sitting. Today Susan had stayed at home with Lloydie, so Mandy was free to join the other girls.

"Church will be at our place next time," she reminded the circle of friends gathered in a bedroom.

"We heard it. Do you think we're deaf?" Lydia remarked.

Mandy looked crestfallen.

"Come on," her friend Alma suggested. "We can go some place else to talk."

As Mandy, Alma, and two other girls left the room, Lydia called after them, "Good riddance!"

"*Ach*, that Lydia," Alma comforted Mandy, "don't mind her. She doesn't like anyone except herself. And I'm not so sure about that."

"I know one thing," Lovina Kline told the other girls. "If Lydia Yoder keeps acting like such a *Naaseweis* (smarty), she'll soon find herself without friends."

"Oh, I don't know about that," Erma Slabaugh replied. "Effie Eash sticks to her pretty good."

"*Ya*, like a cocklebur," Mandy quipped.

This brought peals of laughter. Soon the four friends were sharing happenings of the past week.

"I must tell you what my brother Lloydie did," Mandy said. She told about her trouble at the clothesline. "He follows me all the time. First when he was born, I was so happy. But now I get tired of taking care of him. Mom calls him one of God's special children. Lloydie couldn't come today 'cause he has a cold. Susan stayed at home to watch him."

"Well, we think he is cute, in his own way, even if he's different, don't we girls?" Lovina declared.

"Oh, yes," Alma agreed. "You should see what all my little sister gets into. Last week one night when I was taking the ash box out to empty it, I set it on the floor for a second. Just as I shut the *Offedeer* (stove door), I heard a noise. When I turned around, I saw the ash box upside down and ashes scattered all over. She even put some in her mouth."

That made Mandy feel better even though she knew she shouldn't rejoice in other people's troubles. At least her brother wasn't the only one to get into things.

A good part of the trip home, Mandy talked about the upcoming church service at their house. She also shared the story about Alma's sister and the ashes.

"Du bist un Schnepper box (you're a chatterbox)!" her dad declared. "Do you remember any of today's sermon?"

Mandy became quiet and tried hard to remember. Only one thing came to her mind. Early in his sermon, the minister had said, "We have gathered here to worship the Lord." From there on, she had let her mind wander.

She had seen Roman Kurtz Katie take little Benny to the washhouse. *Probably for a good* Bletsching *(spanking) already,* Mandy figured. Benny had been whining and fussing. It did cause a disturbance, but it seemed rather early in the service for a Bletsching.

As she let her eyes wander, she had seen that Lydia was wearing a new dress. The lady of the house had a huge fern plant displayed by her kitchen window. Then Susie Ropp's baby had dropped her rattle, and quite a few women had jumped at the noise it made. So Mandy's mind had wandered, following her eyes.

"Well," her dad asked again, "what did the minister talk about today?"

Quickly Mandy thought of a safe response. "Why, Dad, he talked about God. Did you forget?"

"No, Mandy, I didn't forget. I only wanted to see if you did."

"We did hear a touching sermon," her mother added. "And our daughter is right. It was about God and God's great love for us."

Mandy breathed a sigh of relief. Yet a twinge of guilt crept into her heart. Tonight she would ask God to forgive her and help her do better. Right now, though, she was listening to her parents' comments.

"After church at our place, I may not hear a sermon for a while," Mother told her husband. "So I'm especially glad for such a good one today."

"Ya, I understand," Dad replied.

"Why, Mom?" Mandy asked. "Why won't you hear a sermon for a while? Will you have to stay home with Lloydie? Won't he get better?"

"No, it's not about Lloydie. Now don't be such a Schnepper box."

Mandy was quiet the rest of the drive home, but her mind was in a whirl.

12
Thanks, Barbara!

What a busy week it was for the Schrock family. The entire house had to be cleaned. Silverware and pots and pans were scrubbed and polished to a shine. All this and more in preparation for the upcoming church service at their place. Even with four older sisters at home yet, Mandy had extra duties assigned.

As soon as she returned from school on Thursday, she heard, "*Mach schnell* (hurry up), Mandy, and change to your chore clothes. You can eat a half-moon pie, then start raking leaves from the front lawn. Take Lloydie with you. He can play outdoors a while. It will be good for him. Give him some pie, too."

"Come on, Lloydie," Mandy said. Her brother grinned that crooked smile and awkwardly followed her to the pantry. He was so happy to see his sister. Mandy could not help but feel his affection, and it touched her.

"You are a bother," she told him, "but in your own

way, you're cute. Wait here till I run upstairs and change. I'll be right back."

"Dee-Dee! Dee-Dee!" Lloydie cried while Mandy was upstairs. He couldn't understand why his sister left him. Mother and Father had said they must all try to teach Lloydie as much as he could grasp. Some things were just too complicated for him. It took lots and lots of patience, and sometimes Mandy felt she had none left.

After Mandy changed, she took Lloydie's hand. "Come on. Now I want you to be good and play with Teddy. Mom wants me to rake leaves." Teddy was Lloydie's favorite toy—an old, raggedy teddy bear with one eye missing.

Mandy brought the lawn rake from the shop, closed the gate, and sat her brother on the porch swing. "*Doh nau* (here now), you swing Teddy." She gave the swing a push to get it going.

At first, this was great. Then Lloydie saw the pile of leaves and the swing lost its appeal. Dragging Teddy by one arm, Lloydie left the porch and ambled toward the inviting leaf pile.

Mandy had worked her way toward the road, gathering some stray leaves. She failed to notice what was about to happen. Then she heard her brother's giggling and the crunching of dried leaves, so she turned around.

"*Ach du* (oh you)!" she exclaimed. "*Du bist en nixnutz* (you're a good-for-nothing)! I can't turn my back one minute. Look at what you did."

The neat pile of leaves which Mandy had raked together was scattered. Lloydie was walking around in the leaves and laughing at the sound they made under his feet. It looked like fun, and Mandy would have been delighted to jump in the pile herself. But then she would need to work harder to undo the damage.

"I'm taking you indoors," she told her brother. Reluctantly he left as his sister led him along. "If I don't hold you by the hand," she grumbled, "you always get in trouble."

"*Was kommt schunnt doh* (what comes here already)?" Mother asked as Mandy entered with Lloydie.

"Ach, Mom," Mandy exclaimed, "I can't rake leaves with Lloydie. He scattered the ones I had gathered all over the grass again. He won't stay on the porch and play with his teddy. Can't you keep him inside?"

"Mom," Barbara suggested, "why don't we let Mandy take Lloydie out and let them both play in the leaves? I'll be glad rake them next week. We'll have time yet before church Sunday.

"Naomi Byler told me she would like to come and help prepare for church. We can rake them then. Mandy takes care of Lloydie a lot, so can we just let them play this one time?"

Naomi was Barbara Schrock's best friend. They enjoyed doing things together. Work didn't seem a burden when they shared it.

Mandy waited for her mother's answer. She hardly dared hope.

"Well, this once I guess it's all right. Lloydie seldom gets to do things other children enjoy. Now you must not forget about your chores, Mandy. Come when you are called," Mother reminded her.

"Oh, I won't forget, Mom. I'll come right away," she promised, taking her brother and returning outdoors.

What fun the two youngsters had. Mandy would build up a bunch of leaves, and then they tumbled and squealed in delight. This was one time she thoroughly enjoyed her brother.

"I don't have to watch that you don't get into mischief this time. You can scatter these leaves all you want to."

Taking a handful, Mandy tossed them into the air. The wind caught every leaf and carried them away. As they fluttered to the ground, Lloydie tried to catch them.

"Thanks, Barbara," Mandy said as she was called to her chores. "Thank you. You're a good sister."

Her heart felt lighter as she went about her duties.

13

For Mom and Lloydie

Things were buzzing in the Schrock household that Friday. Naomi Byler and her mother had come by, like good neighbors, to help with whatever needed doing before Sunday.

Several days earlier, Grandpa Schrocks had come for the day and helped here and there to prepare for Sunday.

Now Grandma Hildie was in the Schrock kitchen to bake the church cookies. These would be passed around for younger children during the three-hour services.

Soda crackers and cool drinks of water would also be offered. The snacks helped to tide the little ones over until the simple after-service meal was served. The youth and adults just waited for lunch.

Hildie's husband, Daniel, also came. Grandpa Weaver was getting along in years but could still work more than many his age.

"You know, *Dawdy* (Grandpa)," Lloyd told his father-in-law, "I'm thinking I may need to take up residence in the barn."

"*Fer was so* (why so)?" Grandpa Weaver asked.

The men were just ready to leave the kitchen. Lloyd looked around at the busy women and made sure they heard what he had to say.

"There's been such scrubbing and *butzing* (cleaning) going on in here. What if they start in on me? Why, they're liable to wash the skin right off my face! I can't wear my shoes inside anymore. *Was soll ich duh* (what shall I do)?" he asked in mock pity.

The men laughed at their pretended predicament as they edged toward the door.

"*Ach, raus mit eich* (oh, out with you both)!" Hannah exclaimed as she waved them onto the porch. "You're just in the way of women who have work to do. You know it's not that bad. Would you want me to have a *schlabbich* (sloppy) house?"

"You with a schlabbich house?" Lloyd exclaimed good-naturedly as he made his way outdoors. "*Sell sei mol der Daag* (that would be the day)!"

"Ach, the men always have to tease," Grandma Hildie commented. "I know I taught you better than to let things be all messed up."

Mandy was always happy when either *Dawdies* (set of grandparents) came. They often brought small treats. Sometimes it was a stick of gum, wintergreen candy, or a pretty hanky. Even if they didn't bring anything extra, she was glad to see them. Today was no exception. As the girls walked down the lane, returning from school, they saw the buggies.

"Grandpas must be here," Esther exclaimed as she started to run.

"*Dawdies*," Mandy shouted, passing her sister. She burst into the house. "*Mammi* (Grandma), *ich bin so froh dich zu sehne* (I'm so glad to see you)."

"Well now, I'm delighted to see you girls, too, but you almost scared me when you came in so *schnell* (quickly)."

"Um, those cookies smell so good. May we have one?" Mandy asked.

"See what your mom says," Grandma Hildie answered.

"Where is Mom?" Esther wondered.

"She and Nettie Byler are working upstairs. I guess she'll be glad to hear you're home. Lloydie needs someone to take care of him so she can get more done."

Mandy could guess who that someone would be. She made her way upstairs.

"Mom," she said, "may I have a cookie? And may I help Mammi bake them?"

"Take Lloydie downstairs, and you and he may each have a cookie. But you can't help bake this time. We're all so busy, and we need you to take care of your brother."

"Why can't Esther take care of him this time?" complained Mandy.

"Esther needs to take all my things out of the china cabinet, clean the shelves, and put new shelf paper in place."

"See how happy your little brother is to see you!" Nettie Byler remarked.

Mandy wondered why everyone thought it was always her duty to care for Lloydie just because he followed her around so much. Yet she did as she was told and carried him downstairs. He was heavy for such a slender girl. Although Lloydie could walk fairly well, Mother didn't want him climbing stairs because he easily fell.

Grandma Hildie was removing the last sheet of cookies from the oven. She had given Esther, Mandy, and Lloydie each one.

"Now," she suggested, "why don't you take your brother out to the porch swing. As soon as I finish up here, I'll join you. I'm getting rather tired, and we can have a good visit."

This sounded good to Mandy. Taking Lloydie and his teddy, she settled next to him on the swing. She kicked the floor, and they started to swing back and forth. Lloydie was gurgling with delight.

Mandy's mother had a beautiful canary bird. Today she had put the cage outside since the weather was nice. The canary's singing always excited Lloydie. He loved it and clapped his hands with glee. Often Mandy would sing to get Tweety started.

"Want Tweety to sing?" she asked. Looking up to the cage, where it hung from the edge of the porch roof, she noticed something was wrong. The cage door was open! No bird was in sight!

"Mammi, *kumm schnell* (come quickly)!" Mandy called.

Fearing something had happened to Lloydie, Grandma came as fast as she could. *"Was is letz* (what's wrong)?"

"Tweety's gone. The cage door's open, and he's no where around. What will Mom say?"

"Bring Lloydie. We'll look around the bushes for the canary," Grandma proposed.

The canary was not in sight anywhere. That evening the entire family searched and searched, but to no avail.

"Will he come back, Dad?" Mandy asked.

"Maybe, if the cat didn't get him."

What a dreadful thought!

That night at her bedside, Mandy prayed, "Please let Tweety come back, for Mom and Lloydie."

14
Tweety Is Back!

Sleep did not come easily the night Tweety disappeared. Mandy wasn't sure if she had latched the cage door. It was her job to keep the birdcage clean and see that the canary had plenty of seed and water.

Once before, Tweety left the cage when she had failed to secure the little hook on his door. That time the cage was inside, and in just a matter of minutes, they caught him. But now he was outside, and Grandpa Weaver said tame canaries can't live long outdoors.

And, oh, horror of horrors! To think a cat might have eaten him! Mandy tossed and turned. She knew there were many cats prowling around the farm.

Tomorrow, church would be at their place. Mandy was happy about that, but she couldn't be completely happy because Tweety was missing.

"Why do you *rutscht rum* (squirm around) so?" Esther asked. "I've been sleeping several times, but you wake me with your rutsching."

"I can't sleep."

"Why not?"

"Tweety is gone, and I think it's my *Schuld* (fault)," Mandy replied.

"How could it be your fault?"

"I think maybe I didn't close his cage door right. Lloydie was following me around, and I got in a hurry. It's hard to do the everyday chores when I want to help with extra stuff to get ready for *Gmee* (church). Oh, I really think I was too *schusslich* (careless)."

"Well, we can't do anything about that now. Go to sleep."

Mandy nestled down under the warm covers.

"Think of nice things. That might help," Esther sighed.

Mandy did try to take her sister's advice. Soon she slept. But what a troubled sleep it was! In her dream, hundreds of yellow canaries were flying through the air. Hundreds of cats were chasing them. All but one little bird escaped. It was Tweety.

"Come on, sleepyhead. Get up." Esther was gently shaking Mandy.

"What! Is it time to get up already? It's still so dark out. Are you sure it's time?"

"Of course I'm sure. No wonder you don't want to get up. You spent half the night rolling around and talking in your sleep."

"Did not!" Mandy protested.

"Did too!" Esther insisted. "Now come on. Did you forget? We're having church here today. That's why we're getting up early. Mom says she wants everything in place before Lewis Krofts get here."

On her way downstairs, Barbara poked her head into Esther and Mandy's room. "Come on, girls, we have a lot to do this morning."

Mandy began to hurry. Wouldn't it be nice if she could help set the tables for the after-church lunch? According to custom, they had made preparations for setting out a simple meal after the service. The older girls always helped with the task. There would be food and lots of visiting.

"Do you think today I could help with the *Middaagesse* (noon meal)?" Mandy asked Esther. They made their way downstairs.

"I doubt it," her sister answered. "Ask Mom. We older girls do that work. Your job is to watch Lloydie. He likes you so much."

There it was again! She could never do what other girls did. It was always the same: Watch Lloydie. Mandy didn't think it was fair. Mother confirmed the fact that Lloydie would be her responsibility for the day.

Sensing her daughter's disappointment, Hannah said, "I won't be going to church for awhile, Mandy. Then you can have more freedom."

Mandy wondered about this but did not comment.

People began to arrive at the Schrock home around eight thirty. Everything was in place, and Hannah was pleased. As usual, Lewis Krofts arrived first, and Lewis Kate (Lewis's wife) began a mental inspection of everything. This did not bother Hannah because she and her girls had the house spick-and-span.

After the singing and Scripture reading with some remarks, the bishop rose to his feet. Standing in the doorway between the living room and kitchen, he greeted the congregation. In his singsong style of preaching, he began his sermon. It was rather warm in the kitchen where the women were seated, so Hannah opened a window just a tad.

Then it happened. Abner Beachy's wife, Mary, let out a shriek—and this was during preaching! There perched upon her white covering sat a bedraggled, yellow canary. He had seen the slightly opened window and was ready to come back home.

Lloydie saw the canary, and it excited him greatly. "Dee-Dee," he chattered.

Mandy tried to shush him, but he rattled on, happy to see their pet. She took Lloydie to the washhouse. Soon her sister Frieda appeared with a frightened canary.

"How did you catch him?" Mandy asked.

"When Abner Mary screeched so, Tweety flew to Lewis Kate's shoulder. She grabbed him. *Nau schnell* (now quick), go bring his cage. We'll keep him out here during church and fellowship time."

Nothing could spoil the day now for Mandy. Tweety was back.

15
Monkey Lloyd

What an exciting Sunday it had been! People joked and laughed about the canary who came to church, spying on their services.

Mary Beachy was embarrassed for shrieking in fright. Hannah was likewise ashamed, but secretly she was glad to have Tweety back. Lewis Kroft's wife felt smug for having caught the intruder.

That noon, waiting for her turn to eat, Mandy was busy entertaining Lloydie. He loved to play with spoons and a plastic bowl. They were sitting in a corner of the living room where they could watch the people. Lloydie's antics did not disturb anyone here.

"Lloydie, I wish I wouldn't always need to watch you. The other girls are upstairs *botsching* peas porridge (playing a rhythmic hand-slapping game), but I have to stay with you."

Lloydie just dumped the spoons out of the plastic bowl and smiled. Many people stopped by and patted

Lloydie's head or told Mandy she was a good girl. After the first tables had been served, Barbara made her way to her sister.

"Mandy, you go eat now. I'll take care of Lloydie and help him with lunch."

"*Danki* (thanks)." Mandy didn't need to be told twice. Quickly she made her way upstairs. There she found her true friend, Alma.

"I can go and eat now," Mandy told her. "Are you ready?"

"Yes," Alma answered. "I was hoping we could eat together."

The two girls were joined by Erma Slabaugh and Lovina Kline. "Do you care if we tag along?" Erma asked. "Effie and Lydia are not fun to be with."

"They talk about other people and make such fun of some," Lovina told the other girls. "We'd rather eat with you, if you don't mind."

"I sure don't mind. Do you, Alma?" Mandy responded.

"Of course I don't," Alma assured them.

"Let's sit by a window table so we can see buggies leave," Mandy suggested. She loved the outdoors, horses, and animals. Today she wanted to see who left early and who stayed.

"Will you be watching your brother again after you have eaten?" Erma asked.

"*Ya*, Barbara told me to come get him as soon as I'm finished eating."

"Well, I'll come with you," Alma promised Mandy.

"Me, too," Lovina remarked.

"So will I," offered Erma. "That is, if it's all right."

"Why wouldn't it be?" Mandy welcomed her. "I'd like it. You know what? There would be four of us. That's just enough for botsching partners."

After eating their fill of hot bean soup, peanut butter spread on thick slices of homemade bread, pickles, and red beets, the girls left the table.

"I'm back," Mandy announced. Barbara was waiting with one of her friends.

"Oh, fine," Barbara responded as she placed Lloydie's hand in Mandy's hand.

"We'll take Lloydie out on the porch for awhile. He may be more content there. I believe so many people make him nervous," Mandy told her friends. Gladly she took her brother outdoors. It was getting too stuffy inside with so many people milling around.

Soon the girls had two games of peas porridge hot going. Whenever they missed a beat in their clapping, they would laugh happily and start over again.

Lloydie seemed to enjoy the fun. He was clapping his own hands, laughing, and giggling.

"This is much more fun than listening to Lydia and her bunch," Erma commented.

"What were they talking about this time?" Mandy asked.

Lovina wished Erma had not mentioned it. She was afraid Mandy would question them.

"For one thing, she talked about your mother opening the window, and the disturbance the canary caused."

"How was my mom to know that the canary was out there? Anyway, I'm just glad he came back. You said for one thing. What else did she say?"

"You know how she is." Alma was trying to distract Mandy. She didn't want her pressing the questions.

"Tell me what Lydia said," Mandy begged.

Fortunately for Erma and Lovina, Lloydie fell off the swing and needed help. The subject concerning Lydia and her remarks was forgotten.

The Schrock girls wanted a young folks' singing that evening. This would be a main social event for Amish youth. As usual, it was to be held at the home where services were held.

Mandy was too young to participate. She did enjoy listening to the hymns. Lloydie had fallen asleep, so Mandy settled down with a bowl of popcorn next to her parents.

"*Sie singe so schnee* (they sing so beautiful)," Mandy remarked.

"Ya," Father agreed, "*awwer nau is Bettszeit* (but now it's bedtime)."

Mandy thought it was the perfect ending of a day. Then as she placed her prayer cap on the dresser, she saw it. Her own autograph book lay open, and written in bold letters was a cruel rhyme:

Mandy can't play the games we enjoyed.
She has to take care of Monkey Lloyd.

"I know who did this!" she cried to Esther. "It was Lydia. And my brother is *not* a monkey!"

16
A New Name

"Stop your crying," Esther told Mandy as they prepared for bed. "Lydia isn't worth being so upset about."

"But it's what she called Lloydie that upsets me," Mandy answered. "Anyway, I'm telling Mom in the morning. She had no right calling him a name."

"Do you suppose that will help? Would it change that girl?"

"Maybe not, but Mom could tell Lydia's mother. Then she might get the *Bletsching* (spanking) she deserves," Mandy figured.

Esther responded thoughtfully. "Lydia needs a change of heart, not a Bletsching."

"She needs a good Bletsching, too," insisted Mandy.

"Well, if you'll be quiet now, I'll let you listen at the window to the *Yunge* (young folks) who are slow leaving the singing. Maybe we'll find out who is taking whom home tonight. Blow out the light so they can't see us watching."

Quickly Mandy extinguished the dim flame in the kerosene lamp and joined her sister. This was exciting! For the moment, Mandy forgot Lydia and her unkind act.

To the girls' disappointment, only a few of the younger boys remained. They were the sixteen-year-olds who had just begun their years of *rumschpringing* (running around with the young folks).

"*Ach*," Mandy whispered, "it's only a bunch of flashlight Simmies."

"*Now* who's calling names?" Esther reminded her sister.

"But that's different. Everyone knows they go by that name. Why do people call them that, anyway?" Mandy asked.

"Because they want to act important and appear tough, but don't know how. They carry big flashlights and shine them on others as they leave the singings, especially the girls. If they shine them in their eyes, it blinds them for a bit.

"As the girls giggle and try to avoid them, the boys swagger and make boastful remarks. They think it's especially great sport to turn their flashlights on a couple trying to make a secret getaway."

"Well, I think they are *gegisch* (silly)," Mandy decided.

"I couldn't agree more," Esther responded. "You know what they remind me of? Like young strutting roosters that don't know how to crow!"

Mandy laughed, and suddenly a half-dozen bright

flashlights turned their beams through their window. Both girls jumped in fright and ran for their bed. Just as they got under the covers, they heard one of the boys say, "Whoever listens behind the wall will hear their own fault."

However, to their disappointment, the girls had not heard anything.

"I bet those boys think they're smarter than ever for scaring us," Mandy remarked.

"Let them think what they will. Now try to get some sleep."

Mandy's thoughts kept returning to the events of the day and the rude note in her autograph book. *Why do we have a boy like Lloydie?* she wondered. As the tears began to come again, she whispered to herself, "Oh, I wish he'd never been born."

At last, sleep came, and with it a dream. A dream of many thoughtless boys and girls pointing at Lloydie and yelling over and over, "Monkey Lloyd! Monkey Lloyd."

Mandy tried to chase them away, but they laughed all the more and yelled louder.

"Mandy, wake up." Esther was shaking her sister, trying to arouse her. "*Was is letz* (what's wrong)? Why are you thrashing about so? You were saying, '*Schtobb, Schtobb graad nau!* (stop! stop right now).' You must have been having a bad dream."

"I was, and I'm glad it was only a dream."

"Do you want to tell me about it?"

"A lot of mean boys and girls were pointing at Lloydie and calling him 'Monkey Lloyd.' Guess who was the ringleader," Mandy said.

"Oh, I suppose it was Lydia. Don't let it bother you so. Lloydie isn't being hurt by name-calling. He doesn't even understand it. Lydia Yoder is only harming herself. Someday she'll be sorry for her actions."

"Well, I'm still telling Mom," Mandy declared. For the second time, she wished Lloydie had never been born.

True to her plan, Mandy told her mother what Lydia wrote in her autograph book.

"Mandy," Hannah counseled, "we must not let what others say cause hard feelings."

"But, Mom, you don't know how that hurt," her daughter answered.

"Yes, I am afraid I do. You see, people have made unkind remarks to me, too."

"Like what?" Mandy wondered.

"Some people asked if perhaps there was someone of the *Freindshaft* (relatives) like Lloydie, and whether he inherited it. They implied that because my mother was adopted, someone in her family might have had Down's syndrome."

"What's Down's syndrome?"

"It's the new name for a mongoloid child. God gave us Lloydie to love and care for. We must remember that. That's all that really matters."

A new name! Mandy would tell Lydia that her brother was not a monkey or a mongoloid. Once more she felt better.

17

A Very Sick Boy

Hannah Schrock had not gone to church for several Sundays. Lloydie stayed at home, too, so Mandy had more freedom to spend time with her friends at the biweekly services and fellowship time.

"Today I'm telling that stuck-up Lydia that my brother is *not* a monkey, and she shouldn't call him a mongoloid," she told Alma, Erma, and Lovina.

"Why, I thought the doctor said he *was* a mongoloid," Lovina replied.

"He did. But then he told mom that now they call it Down's syndrome. So Lydia Yoder can't call him *monkey* anymore," Mandy gloated in triumph.

"Don't worry!" Erma warned. "If I know Lydia, she'll call him whatever she want's to. Maybe she'll think of another name."

"We aren't going to let her spoil our good times together," Alma told the girls.

"My mom said I'm old enough to wear a *Halsduch*

un *Schatz* (cape and apron), like my older sisters do," Mandy informed her friends. "Barbara is making one for me this week. By next church Sunday, I'll be dressed like the big girls."

Mandy knew she shouldn't be proud. She had a hard time not showing it. If she had to struggle so now, how would it be when she actually wore them? But this was an important milestone for her.

"Oh, Mandy," replied Alma, "what a surprise! I'm also wearing my first grown-up outfit in two weeks. So we'll be grown-up together!"

"Oh, goody!" Mandy rejoiced.

"Maybe my mom will let me wear a *Schatz un Halsduch*, too, if I tell her you girls are allowed to," Lovina said wistfully.

"I'm going to ask my mom if she'll make mine, too," promised Erma.

"Wouldn't that be fun if all four of us came in two weeks with our white organdy outfits?" Mandy suggested.

"It sure would," the girls chimed together and then giggled in anticipation.

"I just guess that Lydia and her bunch would be jealous," Mandy remarked.

Mandy knew she should not feel this way. She had been well taught that pride and jealously were wrong. Her parents had told her she must not seek revenge for Lydia Yoder's thoughtlessness.

However, Mandy was young. The community in which she lived would shape her character. Eventually she would mature and submit to Amish standards of humility in spirit, not just in wearing plain dress.

Mandy told Lydia that she shouldn't call Lloydie a mongoloid.

"Sure, I hear you," Lydia smirked. "What is he then, a chimp?"

"No," Mandy answered. "He's a real person, and what he has is called Down's syndrome."

"Oh, so he's a drone!" Lydia mocked. "He looks like one with that odd-looking face." Lydia and her friends laughed uproariously.

"Come on, Mandy," Alma urged, taking Mandy's arm. "Let's go."

After they moved off, Alma soothed Mandy. "My mom says we should pity those girls and pray for them."

When the family came home, Lloydie did not come to meet Mandy as he usually did.

"Where's Lloydie?" Dad asked.

"He seems to have a fever, Lloyd," Hannah told her husband. "Most of the forenoon, he lay beside the stove and slept. If it weren't Sunday, I'd say we should call the doctor."

"Well," suggested Dad, "did you do anything to lower his temperature?"

"I gave him some baby aspirin. Maybe after a good, long nap, he'll feel better. It's so hard to know what to do since he can't tell us where he hurts."

"When he gets up, I'll have a look at him," Dad declared.

Since Lloydie was sick, Mandy had the rest of the afternoon to herself until chore time. She had more chores now because her older sister Susan had married Roman Troyer and had her own home now.

Frieda was spending the day with her boyfriend, Samuel, and his family. People said they would get married before long. Of course, Freida pretended she was visiting his sister, but folks knew better.

Barbara and Ruth decided to walk to the neighbor's and visit their girls. Esther was a bookworm, so she spent the rest of the afternoon reading.

There were so many things Mandy wanted to do. First she went to the barn and played with the *Busslin* (kittens). She decided to walk back to the pond and feed the ducks. On her way she picked wildflowers and watched for birds.

Finally she returned to the house, made herself comfortable with a mail-order catalog, and wished for many things as she turned the pages. *Why can't every day be like this?* she thought. *No Lloydie to take care of!* Yet she did not want him to be sick.

The afternoon passed too quickly, and soon it was chore time. Lloydie was awake, but he seemed worse, Mother observed. His face was flushed, and he whimpered so pitifully. Mother had been bathing him with a cool wet washcloth, but he was still feverish.

Mandy helped Mom give him some sips of fluid since he seemed so hot and dry. But nothing seemed to help.

"I think we'd better send Frieda and Barbara over to Coles to call Dr. Gray," Dad decided.

Mother agreed.

Since they were Amish and thus without a telephone, the girls quickly hitched up the horse and buggy. They drove to the nearest *englisch* (non-Amish) neighbor's house to place the call for Dr. Gray.

The good doctor came, but after examining Lloydie, he was puzzled. "Mr. Schrock," he said, "I can't quite put my finger on the problem here. Lloydie does have a fever, so there must be some infection. Has the boy been coughing, or has he been sick to his stomach?"

"I've been giving him little sips of chicken broth and sweetened mint tea," Hannah reported. "But he hasn't eaten all day, so his stomach has not been upset. There seems to be a dry cough bothering him."

"Then I expect it's a lung infection. I'll leave this antibiotic medicine to fight it and get his fever down. Give him a teaspoonful every four hours.

"I'll be back in the morning. He's a very sick boy," the doctor declared. "But a child can appear serious one minute and better the next. Watch him, and I'll be back."

18
Grief and Peace

True to his word, Dr. Gray did come back the next morning. But his services were no longer needed. Little Lloydie had peacefully slipped away during the night.

Mandy had been awakened by voices in her room. She saw Ruth and Barbara standing there, crying softly.

"How shall we tell her?" Ruth asked.

Mandy sat bolt upright. "Tell who what? Why are you crying?" She saw that Esther's place next to her in bed was empty. "Where's Esther, and what's wrong?" she demanded.

"Esther has gone downstairs," Barbara told her. "She was already awake when we came in to tell her." Barbara struggled to control her emotions.

"What did you tell her? It must be something *schlimm* (serious) or you wouldn't cry," Mandy remarked.

"Come here," Ruth invited. She put her arms around her sister, something she had never done before. Mandy was frightened. Now she knew for sure that something drastic had happened.

As gently as they could, the two girls broke the news of Lloydie's death to Mandy.

"You mean he's gone forever?" she asked in shocked disbelief.

"Yes, Mandy. From this life here, he is gone forever," Barbara confirmed.

"But the doctor said he would come back. He could make Lloydie well again. That's what doctors do, isn't it?" Mandy groped to understand what had happened.

"Well, yes, if it's God's will. The doctor did come *frieh den Maryie* (early this morning), but God's angel had already taken our Lloydie to heaven."

"*Ich kann's net glaawe* (I can't believe it)," Mandy declared.

"Get dressed, and we'll take you to see him. Put on your brown school dress," Barbara told her. "People will be coming to help out, so you need to wear suitable clothes."

"But Mom never let's me wear a school dress to do my chores," Mandy reminded them.

"You won't be doing your chores for a few days," Ruth assured her.

"Who will do them, then?" Mandy wondered as she put on her school clothes.

"Our neighbors and friends. That's the way our people do at a time of loss. Come now. Mother will wonder what's keeping us."

Mandy did not like the atmosphere of the living

room this morning. Instead of the usual hustle and bustle, it was quiet. Her mother sat in her rocker, crying.

She noticed her father wiping tears from his eyes also. Mandy had never seen her dad cry. It made her feel sad and scared. Her father had always seemed like a tower of strength, and now he was crying. What was happening to her parents?

"Take Mandy in to see him before the undertaker comes," Mother told the girls. According to Amish custom, they would keep their departed loved one in their home until the time for burial.

Mandy followed her sisters into the downstairs spare bedroom. This had been Lloydie's bedroom.

"Why, he looks like he's just asleep," Mandy observed. "See!" She reached out to touch him. "Lloydie, *wacker warre* (wake up)." But he was cold to her touch and did not respond. Now she knew. "*Welle naus geh* (let's go out)," she told her sisters.

Two of the neighbor men and their wives were already there to assist. Lloyd went to the barn with the men to instruct them and acquaint them with the choring routine.

The women soon had breakfast ready, but no one felt like eating. All day long, people kept coming. Since the body was at the house, calling hours were anytime. During the night, a wake was observed. Several people stayed awake in the room with the body all night.

The bishop and other ministers came. They asked the family if they had a special Scripture passage they wished to be used. What hymns did they want to have sung or read? Who did they name as pallbearers?

Mandy was too young to take part in these decisions. One thing she did request. Could they let Lloydie take his raggedy teddy bear to his grave?

"He needs him, Mom," she begged. "He'll miss him, I know he will."

This would be highly unusual for an Amish burial. But Mandy fretted about it so much that Father finally consented to speak to the bishop.

"Lloyd, you know this is not our way. We brought nothing into this world, and it is certain we will take nothing out. But I know Jesus cared for *die kleine Kinder* (the little children), and if it helps your little Mandy in her grief, I see nothing wrong with it."

"*Danki* (thank you)" is all Lloyd could say to this kind man.

Thus it came to be that as folks viewed the body of little Lloydie, they saw a well-worn teddy bear cradled in the crook of one arm.

"I like our bishop," Mandy said. "He knew that was the last thing I could give Lloydie."

In her grief, she felt a moment of peace.

19
It's All My Fault

Mandy wished the funeral was over with. She did not like to see her family crying. Many others were shedding tears and blowing their noses. It was such a sad time. To add to the feelings of despair, the weather was dreary and rainy.

Mandy was wearing her new cape and apron outfit for the first time. She had longed for that occasion, thinking how proud and grown-up she would be. It didn't matter anymore. She certainly did not carry any pride in her heart today. Instead, Mandy felt humbled.

The congregation sang "Gute Nacht ihr, meine Liebe (Goodnight to you, my beloved)" and "Was Gott tut, das ist wohlgetan (What God has done is done aright)." One of the ministers preached a short sermon. Then the bishop stood up and spoke comforting words.

"We are gathered here today not of our own choosing," he said. "God has deemed it best to call one of his children home. This was a different child, but one who touched our hearts in many ways. Although some mocked, sad to say, yet Lloydie was a friend to all who accepted him. He was somewhat limited, but his ready smile touched others.

"God sent him to this earth for a purpose, and I believe we can say we have learned from him. In his short life here, he taught us patience. *Ach,* I'm sure it took patience to care for him. He taught us love. He loved everyone. He taught us kindness. He was gentle with small animals.

"You will notice that he has his favorite stuffed animal, placed in the casket at the request of his youngest sister. This may seem strange, but I ask your understanding for a sister who was his constant companion.

"Yes, Lloydie, as he was known to everyone, has left an impression upon us all. Who of us could have said it would have been better had he never been born? Indeed, by his pleasant ways, he taught us. But then pneumonia set in, and God called our little friend home. We commit his spirit unto God, from whence it came."

The bishop's sermon continued for over an hour, as he spoke of Jesus blessing the children and of hope for resurrection life. After another hymn in German, "Come, Children, Let Us Be Going, The Evening Draws Nigh," preparation was made for burial.

Mandy thought the long drive to the cemetery seemed endless. But she didn't want it to end because that would be the last time she would look upon the face of her departed brother. They would open the casket just before lowering it in the ground, so those present could give Lloydie a last good-bye.

Many friends followed the Schrock family to show their sympathy and support. The rain had stopped, but the ground was soaked.

"How can they close that box and put Lloydie down in that wet, dark hole?" Mandy whispered to her sister, Barbara.

"It's only the shell of his body, Mandy. Lloydie isn't there. He's with Jesus. We must be quiet now." Barbara had noticed people looking at them.

"Come, stand here by me," Frieda told Mandy. She held Mandy's hand, and that helped.

As the casket was closed and began its descent into the ground, people began to sing once more.

Why do they have to sing? Mandy wondered. She certainly didn't feel like singing. Mandy had been to funerals and knew this was their custom. Yet never before had it bothered her. This time it was different because it was her family.

Mandy hated to hear the thud the shovels full of dirt made as they began covering Lloydie's coffin.

"Why do we have to stand here and watch?" she asked Frieda.

Her sister was crying so hard and only squeezed Mandy's hand. Mandy turned her face away and looked right into the face of Lydia Yoder. For the first time, Mandy saw a look of meekness in Lydia's expression.

Suddenly it began to rain hard. Everyone made their way to the buggies. Horses whinnied and stomped the ground, eager to get home. The grave site was covered with a canvas tarp and left until later. The grave diggers took shelter in a small shed that housed the shovels and other tools. They had almost completed their task when the rain poured down.

People began to leave, going back to the Schrock home where a meal had been prepared for all who cared to share with the family. Many did come.

"I wish it wouldn't rain so," Mandy groaned on the way home. "Now Lloydie will get all wet. Why does it rain so hard?"

Mother suppressed a sob, but Father answered, "Perhaps God is sending heaven's tears to blend with our own. He cares that we are hurting."

"But, Dad," Mandy reminded him, "I thought there are no tears in heaven."

"Then maybe God made some to send to earth just for us."

"Well, the bishop preached a wonderful sermon, and it comforted me," Mother said. "*Ach,* I was never sorry that we had Lloydie, not once."

Fear struck Mandy's heart, for she remembered telling her brother that she wished he had never been born.

Oh, it's all my fault. God took Lloydie to punish me. It's all my fault!

Mandy was crushed at that thought.

20
What Could Go Wrong?

Many people followed the Schrock family back to their house. They would share a meal furnished and prepared by caring friends.

Mandy's friends Alma, Lovina, and Erma were also there. They wanted to comfort her but hardly knew how. It just seemed there was nothing to say. Lydia Yoder and her parents had come, too. Even Lydia was at a loss for words.

Finally Alma said only two words to Mandy: "I'm sorry."

Mandy burst into tears. *"Ich bin ein schlimm Meedel* (I'm a bad girl), Alma."

"I didn't mean to make you cry. You're not bad, and we like you, don't we girls?" Alma turned to Lovina and Erma for their affirmation.

"Of course we like you," Erma told Mandy, with warmth and concern in her voice.

"You'll always be our friend," Lovina assured her.

They hadn't noticed Lydia and Effie standing near-by. Now Lydia came to Mandy with a few comforting words: "I'm sorry about your brother, and I'm sorry I made fun of him." Then perhaps to make up for her former rudeness, she added, "You look good in a cape and apron."

Mandy only nodded in recognition.

"*Ya*," Effie agreed, "I think so, too."

This was so out of character for both Effie and Lydia that Mandy did not know how to respond. She was glad for the change but said nothing.

The rain was still falling at chore time. Most families had returned to their own homes and work.

"Mom," Mandy asked, "may I take the umbrella when I go to gather the eggs?"

"You won't be gathering the eggs tonight," Hannah Schrock told her daughter.

"Why not?" She wondered if everything must stop because Lloydie died.

"Come," urged Barbara gently. "Mom's tired. Our neighbors will still chore for us tonight."

"What shall I do then?" Mandy wished she could go outside. The house was such a quiet, sad place tonight.

"If you want to, I'll let you look through my autograph book."

"Oh yes, Barbara, I'd like that!" Mandy exclaimed. Then she added, "But maybe I'm too bad."

"Too bad? Now why would you say that?"

Mandy couldn't tell her.

"Wait here in the living room while I go upstairs and get it," Barbara told her.

The four grandparents were still sitting with Mandy's mother and father, comforting them by just being there.

"Come here, Mandy," Grandma Hildie said. "You took such good care of Lloydie. I know you'll miss him. He really liked you. Remember, where he is now is far better."

In spite of her grandma's kind words, Mandy could only remember how she had sometimes wished that Lloydie had never been born into their family.

"Here." Barbara handed the autograph book to her sister. "Sit by the stove where it's nice and warm, and take your time looking through it."

Mandy opened to the first page and tried to concentrate. Any other time she would have been thoroughly lost in the small book's contents. It had blank colored pages on which friends had written verses, humorous comments, and good wishes. Then they signed their names.

She found one rhyme which caught her interest, but not for long. It was a nice verse, but it made her think of Lloydie.

> I wish you health, I wish you wealth,
>   I wish you gold in store.
> I wish you heaven after death.
>   What could I wish you more?

It was beautiful, but there was that word *death* again, and she didn't like it.

Frieda's boyfriend, Samuel, had helped with the outside work the last few days. He was still there that evening. Frieda and Sam were alone in the kitchen, discussing plans for their future. Susan and her family left because they needed to put their little ones to bed.

Barbara's friend Katie was preparing to leave also. Esther was curled up with a book.

"You look so tired, Hannah," Lloyd told his wife.

"Yes, she does," agreed Lloyd's mother, Grandma Schrock. "I think we'd better go home, too. It doesn't sound as if this rain will let up, so we might as well leave now."

The neighbors brought their horse and buggy to the house for the Schrock grandparents.

A little later, as the Weaver grandparents were departing, Grandma Hildie told her daughter Hannah to take care of herself. "Especially now! We don't want anything to go wrong."

Mandy wondered what Grandma meant. *What might go wrong?* She was frightened. Lloydie was gone. *Is something going to happen to my mother, too?*

"Girls, it's time for you to get some sleep. *Es is hoch Bettzeit* (it's bedtime for sure)."

Mandy did not want to go to bed. She obeyed, but she could not sleep. What could go wrong with her mother?

21

A Secret No More

Esther was sleepy and soon in dreamland. Not so for Mandy. Her thoughts were troubled and all mixed up. She tossed and turned well into the night.

Mandy felt she was bad regardless of what her friends had said. And now something was going to happen to her mother. She just knew it.

"Mandy, will you stop your *rutsching* (squirming)?" Esther protested. "You keep waking me up. Don't you know what time it is?" She glanced at the bedside alarm clock. "It's already one-thirty. Go to sleep, and stop tossing around so much."

"I can't sleep," Mandy admitted.

"*Fer was net* (why not)?" Esther asked.

"I'm a bad girl, Lloydie is gone, and something's going to happen to Mom," Mandy confessed.

"What makes you say you're bad? And why do you think something will happen to Mom?"

Mandy ignored the first question. Her answer to

the second one seemed to amuse Esther. "I heard Grandma Weaver tell Mom to take care of herself. She said, '*Fer schur nau* (especially now), we don't want anything to go wrong.' "

"*Ach,* Mandy," chuckled Esther "don't you know what she meant?"

"No." Mandy was annoyed at Esther's reaction. "I don't think it's funny."

"Haven't you noticed that Mom isn't going along to church lately?"

"She was staying home watching Lloydie," Mandy reminded her.

"That wasn't the only reason. Remember how we used to take turns caring for Lloydie?"

"Well, then what is it?" Mandy asked.

"Before Lloydie was born, Mom stayed home from church. Then after the baby came, she went again. She had to take extra good care of herself before Lloydie was born. Don't you understand why Grandma Weaver said what she did?"

Mandy sat up with a start. "You mean we'll have a new *Buppeli* (baby)?"

"Yes, silly. You don't need to jump out of bed. Be quiet. Do you want to wake the whole household? Anyway, I'm not sure I should have told you. Mom doesn't like for us to know until we are old enough. So let's keep it a secret."

"How old is old enough?" Mandy asked.

"*Ach, du gleene Gwunnernaas* (oh, you little wonder nose), go to sleep! Are you going to talk all night?"

Mandy tried to lie as still as she could. It was not easy. So many things were happening, and thoughts were whirling in her mind. Bishop had said Lloydie was in a better place now. Mandy felt she was bad because she had often been impatient with Lloydie.

Now she was grown-up enough to wear the cape and apron. Lydia and Effie had been nice to her. She didn't even feel proud dressing as a teenager.

Esther had just told her there would be another Buppeli. She wanted to ask Esther whether it would be a girl or boy, but Esther was asleep again.

Mandy wished in her heart for a boy. She knew her dad was so pleased when Lloydie was born. How could Esther lie there and sleep! Mandy decided no matter how much care the new Buppeli took, she would do it gladly. Eventually Mandy slept.

Things began to return to the everyday, normal routine. Mandy was given more duties both indoors and out. She enjoyed outside work and at times found the housework depressing.

Whenever she came in from doing her chores, there was no happy voice calling "Dee-Dee, Dee-Dee." No sound of shuffling feet and a smiling boy coming to meet her. Mandy remained moody and ate little. Even her friends could not get her to join in their fun.

Lydia Yoder and her group had now changed, and things seemed to be going well. It was much more pleasant to gather after the services. The circle of girls Mandy's age could not understand the change in her. She was so quiet and seldom smiled. This was strange for one who used to be the life of the party. No one knew the ache Mandy carried in her heart.

"I'm worried about Mandy," Hannah told her husband. "Have you noticed how thin she's getting?

Whenever she has free time, she goes somewhere to be alone. Usually it's down by the pond where she sits and looks out over the water. I'm sure she misses Lloydie, but I think it must be more than that. The other girls miss him too, but they go on."

Lloyd thought about that for a while, then replied. "We must consider that the care of Lloydie was largely Mandy's responsibility. Perhaps that's why she misses him so."

"Do you think I should tell her there will soon be a new Buppeli in our family? Maybe that will help. I think she's old enough to know."

"Do what you think is best," Lloyd answered.

So it came to be that the secret was a secret no more. Mandy was glad because several times she almost let it slip that she knew. She was happy to be considered old enough.

22

The Lighthouse

Hannah Schrock had hoped that once Mandy knew there would be another *Buppeli* (baby) in the family, she would be happy again. But she remained mysteriously moody.

Even after baby Jonas arrived, Mandy often seemed in a world of her own. Her new brother was healthy and robust. Yes, he was a gut Buppeli, needing little care. Mandy never resented watching him nor would she ever. Not one day passed that her conscience didn't trouble her. If only she could undo the things she had done!

Mandy's mother even took her to see Doctor Gray, but he found no physical illness.

In the next three years, changes came in the Schrock family. Frieda and Ruth were both married. By now, Barbara had been *rumschpringing* (going with the young folks) for two years. She also worked as a *Maut* (hired girl) in other Amish homes.

That left Esther and Mandy at home.

"Soon it'll be your turn to come to singings," Esther told Mandy. Esther had only been rumschpringing for one year.

"I don't think I want to," Mandy informed her sister.

"Well, why not? Do you want to sit at home all your life?"

"Maybe no one would want to sit with me at singings, or eat with me at a box social."

"Don't put yourself down! You won't know until you go," Esther told her. "Box socials are a lot of fun, Mandy. You never know who will buy your lunch or who you'll be eating with. I know you'll like it."

However, Mandy wasn't sure she wanted to try it. Anyway, she wouldn't be sixteen for seven months. She would think about it later.

This was her last year in school since the Amish did not send their children to high school. Her parents had kept her out of school until she was eight years old so the state law would allow her to quit after grade eight.

Miss Zook gave the eighth-grade students a poem to memorize. All six of her pupils were to learn it. She wanted this to be recited at the special year-end program.

"A part will be given to each of you for that day. Awards will be presented, but since there is such short notice to learn the poem, I'll give a special prize to the one who learns it best. And that student will recite the poem at the program. I'll put the words on the chalkboard for you to copy, so get busy."

She knew some of the class would say they couldn't memorize the whole poem, so she offered the special prize to encourage them.

"I'm not even going to try," Elam Mast muttered to his friend Mose Raber.

"*Ya*, anyway, the girls always win. It'll probably be something *kindisch* (childish) that we wouldn't want."

"No whispering," Miss Zook insisted. "You'd better start writing."

The boys began to copy the words even though they had decided not to memorize them:

The Lighthouse

A welcome sight on a dark stormy night
Is the lighthouse on the shore,
To the sailors who follow its beckoning light
That guides them home once more.
Tho' the waves dash high
While the breakers cry,
And the sea is white with foam,
Still onward they sail,
Weathering the gale,
To the lighthouse which guides them home.

We, too, have a lighthouse to show us the way;
'Twill lead us wherever we roam.
Jesus is that Light, our Strength and our Stay;
He safely will guide us on home.
Tho' trials may come, and dark be the night,
And Satan may buffet us sore,
Keep your eyes upon Jesus for He is the light
That will lead us to heaven's fair shore.

The words held Mandy's attention as nothing had for a long time. Not since Lloydie's death had she been so lost in thought. Those words—"Tho' trials may come and dark be the night, and Satan may buffet us sore"! She wondered what the word *buffet* meant. Lydia Yoder also wondered, and she asked Miss Zook.

"It means that something troubles us with great force. Satan does batter us, you know," Miss Zook explained. "He wants us to doubt and be unhappy.

"But children, don't listen to Satan. Jesus knows all our fears. Jesus is Light, Satan is darkness. Satan wants us to think we are so bad that Jesus doesn't care for us. But that's why God sent Jesus, to forgive us and give us a fresh start. He surely will guide us safely home, just as the poem says.

"Now finish your work. It's almost time to dismiss."

Mandy pondered the teacher's words. Hadn't it been her fault that her brother died? Was it possible that Jesus would wipe out her sins?

"Lydia," Mandy confided as they walked home from school. "I'm glad you asked Miss Zook what the word *buffet* meant. I was wondering about it too."

The two girls had become good friends since the day Lydia apologized and asked Mandy's forgiveness.

"Do you think God can forgive me if I've been bad?" Mandy asked.

"Of course. Miss Zook said Jesus is our Light. I never thought of Jesus that way before, but I'm sure Miss Zook knows what's right," Lydia said.

Mandy agreed.

23
The Prize

Mandy's heart felt lighter than it had for a long time. *If I can forgive Lydia, surely God will forgive me,* she reasoned.

"Mom," Mandy began as she set her lunch pail on the table, "Miss Zook gave us a poem to learn for the school program.

"It is called 'The Lighthouse.' Teacher said that all those who learn it will get an award, but the one who gives it at the program will get a special prize. I hope I can learn it well."

"You must try your best then," her mother advised her. "It isn't just the special prize that matters. The discipline and effort you put into it is what really counts. I know you can do it well."

Mandy took her mother's counsel to heart. Every evening she studied the poem. One night after supper Esther asked Mandy to recite it to her.

"Oh, Mandy," she exclaimed, "*sell is so schee* (that's

so pretty)! You say it like you mean it. It sounds as if you're right there. I'm sure you'll get the prize."

Mandy, however, wasn't sure she wanted it. She felt perhaps that she didn't deserve it. At recess time she and some of the girls listened to each other practice. Erma and Alma did it quite well, too.

Finally the last day of school arrived. Now the long-awaited time for the program had come. By three o'clock, the one-room schoolhouse was well filled. Some students gave up their seats for the parents. Other parents and older brothers and sisters were standing around the back of the room.

At Miss Zook's request, they began by singing two German hymns led by one of the fathers. When that was over, a shy first grader gave a welcome to all. Everyone smiled and nodded approval as the nervous little one gave her lines.

"We're glad our program you didn't need to miss, but I'm glad school is over with. Welcome!" She couldn't pronounce the word *program* correctly, but that made it all the more precious. As people clapped, the little girl tried to hide behind her mother.

Next, children from different classes were called upon for various recitations. This gave the pupils a chance to share some of what they had learned during this school term.

"And now," announced Miss Zook, "we have a special treat for you. It was hard to choose from among my eighth graders, as most of them did well. I tried to be fair and, after carefully listening to each one, I have chosen Mandy Schrock. She will come and recite a poem, 'The Lighthouse.' "

No one knew beforehand who would be picked. Mandy could hardly believe that she was the one. She had imagined that her friend Erma would be chosen. Mandy hesitated for a moment.

"Mandy?" Miss Zook called.

Slowly Mandy rose to her feet and made her way to the front of the crowded room. Her throat felt dry. She paused. Then she saw her mother's smiling face and her father watching. That gave her strength. Her mother and Miss Zook had confidence in her. She could not disappoint them!

The words poured forth with such expression as to cause a hush to fall upon the audience. Mandy was totally wrapped up in her recitation.

To everyone's surprise, Elam Mast stood at the chalkboard doing a beautiful colored-chalk drawing of a storm-tossed ship at sea and a lighthouse on the shore. Elam was talented in art, and the teacher had placed him close to the board to avoid distraction.

She had asked Elam to stay after school several times to work on the drawing. No one else knew it was coming, and he kept the secret well.

The combined presentation was a great success. So deeply was Mandy involved in her part that she was not aware of Elam's work at the board until she was finished.

In closing the program, Miss Zook called the eighth graders forward so she could present their awards. To each she gave bookmarks and a pen.

For his work, Elam Mast received a sketchbook and art materials. For Mandy, Miss Zook had a book entitled *God's Unfailing Grace.*

After the eighth-grade class received their diplomas, the entire school sang "Jewels." Miss Zook asked the bishop to dismiss them with a prayer.

Afterward, everyone stood around visiting for a while, men with men, women with women, girls with girls, and boys with boys.

"Oh, Mandy, I'm glad you got the prize!" Erma exclaimed.

"But Erma, I think you should have been the one. You always said the poem better than I did."

"She did it just right, didn't she?" Erma asked the other girls. "You made our whole class look good."

"Oh yes," they agreed.

"It went so well with Elam Mast's drawing," Lydia remarked.

"I didn't even know he was back there," Mandy admitted with a laugh.

The girls chattered happily, lingering with the excitement of their last school activity.

"Miss Zook sure knows how to spring things on us."

"Yes, but *sie is ein gute* (she is a good) teacher."

"May I see your book?" asked Erma.

"Sure." Mandy handed it over.

"It's so pretty. I like the blue cover and gold lettering."

"Erma, I still think you should have it," Mandy told her.

"No, but maybe I'll ask to borrow it sometime, if you don't mind."

"You sure can," Mandy assured her.

"Me, too," remarked Lydia.

"And me," Alma chimed in.

"I'll gladly share," Mandy promised. "Now, did you girls think of it? We've graduated, and that means we won't be seeing each other every weekday like we did at school."

It was a sad thought and yet a happy day. They were moving on in life.

Erma looked ahead. "Well, there will be church Sundays, and we can sometimes visit each other on the no-church Sundays."

"And after a while, we'll be *rumschpringing* (going around with the youths)," Lydia reminded her friends. "Won't that be fun?"

The girls all giggled as they went outside for the end-of-school picnic. Miss Zook supplied bananas, and the mothers had brought potato salad, cold chicken sandwiches, cracker pudding, cakes, cookies, and iced spearmint tea.

As a special treat, a few families had brought hand-cranked freezers of homemade ice cream. Sharing this together was a happy ending to a special day.

Then each family went home to do their evening chores together. On the way, Mandy was holding tight to her new book.

24
Healing Begun

It was a busy summer for the Schrock family. Esther was taking instruction class for baptism. Barbara was getting married in the late fall. Having a wedding meant much extra work.

They needed to put away twice as many cans of fruits and vegetables. Esther and Barbara had purchased material for new dresses. Barbara would wear the traditional blue for her wedding, and Esther's dress would be black.

"Why do we have to can more tomato juice?" Mandy asked her mother.

It was a sultry summer day. Because of the humidity, Mandy's clothes were sticking to her warm body. Sweat beads trickled down her face and dripped from her nose.

"Just keep picking, and soon we can take these tomatoes to the washhouse. It'll be cooler there," Hannah told her daughter.

"We've already put up a lot. Why do we need so much more?"

"Did you forget Barbara is getting married? She'll need to take some along to store in their basement when she sets up housekeeping."

"Then let her come out and pick her tomatoes herself," Mandy grumbled.

"*Ach,* Mandy, she's busy varnishing the living room woodwork and floor. I can't stand doing that job. The smell of varnish makes me sick. Barbara kindly offered to do it for me.

"You know she has two weeks off from her *Maut* (hired girl) job. It won't be long until she leaves home. We need to pull together and be nice to her while she's still with us."

Mandy mumbled something under her breath, too low to be heard properly: "What's wrong with Esther helping?"

"*Was saagst du* (what did you say)?" Mother asked.

"*Nix* (nothing)." Mandy wished she hadn't said anything.

"As soon as your bucket is full, we'll quit. *Die Sunn is hees* (the sun is hot). We'll rest under the maple tree.

"I'll get Esther to bring us some cool lemonade. She's probably ready for a break. This week she had two full baskets of ironing to do. That isn't a comfortable job in this kind of weather either," Hannah Schrock reminded Mandy.

Finally all the tomatoes were gathered and carried to the washhouse. Esther made ice-cold lemonade and took some to the field for her dad and brother.

By evening much had been accomplished through

family teamwork. They all were ready for well-earned rest.

Mandy sat at the kitchen table to read from her new book, *God's Unfailing Grace*. But she was so weary that sleep overtook her, and the book slid from her hands.

"Bettzeit fer schmaertie Leit (bedtime for smart people)," her dad announced with fatherly tenderness as Mandy sat up with a start.

"I don't even have time to read the book Miss Zook gave me," she muttered. "All we do is work, work, work! By evening I'm too tired."

"Mandy, we should be thankful for work," her father urged. "It's a God-given privilege. Sundays are for reading and resting."

"But Sundays, Jonas needs—oh, forget it." She had started to remind her dad that her Sundays were often spent entertaining her baby brother. No, she would not say it! Had not God taken her other brother because she complained?

"I guess I'll have to find another time to read it," she remarked.

Mandy was old enough now that she had begun to understand the German language better. She listened intently as the minister started to speak that Sunday in church.

He preached about God's forgiveness and his forgetfulness. Mandy didn't think God ever forgot anything. But the minister proclaimed, "God does not reward us according to our deeds, but is merciful. His grace is sufficient.

"If we repent, God will remove our sins as far from

us as the east is from the west and remember them against us no more.

"Yes," the preacher declared, "God's grace is unfailing."

Mandy tingled at those words. They were like the title of her book! *Will God really forget the bad things I've done?*

The minister went on to say that if we are truly sorry and confess our sin, it is forgotten.

"Why, then, can we not forget if God can?" he asked.

Could it really be true? Mandy knew the minister did not lie. He was preaching from the Bible, and she knew that was truth.

She must tell someone what she had done. But who? Who would understand? She would tell Mother. *Mother will understand*, she told herself.

After they came home that afternoon, Mandy found a quiet time to sit on the porch swing with her mother. Hannah Schrock listened as Mandy poured out her heart.

"I didn't mean it, Mom," Mandy sobbed. "Did God take little Lloydie because I wished we didn't have him? Because I got tired of taking care of him? Will God forget, like the minister preached today?"

"Oh, Mandy, so this is why you've been troubled so long!" her mom responded. "You were just a child back then. I often think I put too much responsibility on you.

"No, Mandy, God did not take Lloydie because of what you said. He doesn't work that way. God loaned precious Lloydie to us for a brief time. Then it was

Lloydie's time to go, as it will be at one time or another for each of us."

"But Mom, why did Lloydie have to die so soon? He didn't even have a chance to grow up."

"That's true, Mandy, and we are all grieving over that. We enjoyed Lloydie's happy smile, but Down's syndrome brought on health problems for him that shortened his life. There was nothing more we could do."

"So that's what it was," said Mandy. "At least he isn't suffering now, and nobody is making fun of him anymore."

"Yes, that's right. God called him home, and he's safe there."

Her mother added wise counsel: "God's sees your heart and knows you want to become patient in bearing burdens. Leave the past to the mercy of God, and leave today to God's love. If we do that and trust God for what lies ahead, all will be well.

"I've made many mistakes in my life, but I can't dwell on them. Let's go on, forget the past, and leave the rest to God."

Talking out her feelings was just what Mandy needed. Mom *did* understand.

Healing had begun for Mandy.

25
Jumping Off

Mandy loved the afternoons on alternate Sundays when they had no services. After a few household duties, she had some free time. This Sunday her parents and young Jonas had been invited to visit friends for the day.

While cleaning up the breakfast dishes, sweeping the kitchen floor, and feeding the canary, she was planning her day. First she thought about making herself comfortable with a book. But much as she loved to read, she decided to postpone it. The outdoors seemed to be calling her.

First she would take a leisurely walk. Some late wildflowers were dotting roadside banks. Brightly mottled butterflies flitted to and fro, and birds gave forth their trilling notes.

What a beautiful day! In fact, what a beautiful world! Mandy walked on deep in thought until she heard a horse and buggy approaching from behind. *Who could it be?* she wondered. The clip-clop of the horses' hooves drew near and then stopped.

"Want a ride?" the driver asked.

Mandy recognized the voice. "Why, Lydia, where are you going?"

"I was coming to spend the day with you, but if you have other plans . . ."

"No, no, I have no special plans. I'm glad you came," Mandy assured her.

"Climb in, then," Lydia replied.

"Okay." Mandy took her place next to Lydia. "Let's not drive fast. It's such a *schenner Daag* (pretty day)."

Lydia laughed heartily.

"What's so funny?" Mandy asked.

"You are," Lydia told her. "Old Sailor couldn't go fast even if you put dynamite under him."

"No, he probably couldn't," Mandy agreed. "But I bet he'd go farther than he ever did before."

"*Wie so* (how so)?" Lydia inquired.

"It would blow him sky-high!" Mandy exclaimed.

They both giggled at the thought of it.

"Why did you name him Sailor?"

"My brother named him, in fun, just because he's so slow. Are you sure I'm not spoiling your plans?" Lydia asked again.

"Not at all. Everyone is gone for the day. After my walk and some lunch, I might have taken a short nap. Then if I could find something to read, I would do that. But this is so much nicer." Mandy smiled, turning to her friend.

"By the way," Lydia told her, "I brought a book I thought you might like. Erma borrowed it and said she enjoyed it. Reach under the buggy seat. It's in a paper bag."

Mandy soon had the book in her hands, admiring the colors on its cover. "Oh, thank you! It looks so exciting! This title—*The Jumping-Off Place*—sounds interesting. What's it about, Lydia?"

"Oh, no, no fair telling. You must read it for yourself."

"But I don't know if I can wait."

"Then see the back cover. It gives a summary."

Mandy read about a young girl who moved to Oregon with her parents. On the way, they endured many hardships. The girl became angry and resentful toward her father. Later she struggled to find forgiveness.

Chills ran up and down Mandy's back. This sounded so like her hard feelings for having to take care of her brother Lloydie and suffer ridicule.

"Oh, Lydia, did the girl ever find forgiveness?"

"It would spoil the story if I told you everything. But check the bottom of the cover. See, it says 'Mae found peace at the jumping-off place.' "

"But how did she? What must I do—?" Mandy broke off when she realized what she had said.

"What are you talking about?"

"*Ach*, we are almost at my house. We'll talk about it after lunch," Mandy answered. Now that this much had been said, she could hide it no longer from her friend.

The girls had a delicious meal of ham sandwiches, potato salad, ice-cold lemonade, fresh peaches, and cake.

"Let's sit on the porch swing," Mandy suggested.

"It's shady here when the sun is so warm."

That's where they spent the afternoon and where Mandy poured her heart out to Lydia.

"*Ach*, Mandy, I often wondered why you were sad. It surely isn't your fault that Lloydie died."

"How do you know?" Mandy wondered.

"Once I was angry with my older sister. To her face I told her I wished we never had her. But God didn't take her from us. One day I told her how sorry I was, and she did forgive me.

"If Lloydie were still living and could understand, I'm sure he'd do the same."

"Yes," Mandy responded, "I guess he couldn't grasp what I was struggling with."

"You know how happy he was around you. You took care of him a lot. God saw that and will forgive you for resenting the burden."

"Well, thanks for listening. I feel so much better after talking this out."

"Now I know why I was supposed to come and visit you today," added Lydia. "Isn't it strange? Long ago, we didn't like each other. Now we're best friends. If we can forgive each other, I'm sure God forgives, too. His love is much greater than ours."

"You're so understanding," Mandy said.

"We give up the cruel deeds we've done. It's like in Mae's life in the story *The Jumping-Off Place*. Her mother told her that when God buries the hatchet, he doesn't leave the handle exposed. Our mistakes are buried in the sea of God's forgetfulness.

"We don't need to blame ourselves any longer. I'm sure you'll find the peace you're looking for."

"Oh, I'm so glad you came. Now I see that I've been fighting myself. Why should I keep bringing up the past when God doesn't?"

The girls visited some more and talked of their upcoming period of *rumschpringing* (going around with the youth).

Mandy felt happier than she had for a long time. She had heard the same truth from the bishop and from Lydia: God does forget if we are truly sorry and change. And Mandy truly was sorry.

As Lydia prepared to leave, she had a few last words for Mandy.

"Let me know how you like the book I'm loaning you. Once your mind is at peace, I think we too are ready for jumping off! It's about time for us to start going around with the young folks."

Mandy knew she was finding peace. Lydia had helped her, and their friendship would be a lasting one. How light her heart felt!

26
The Letter

The mail carrier was early today. Mandy saw his car pull away from the mailbox. Eagerly she put down her half-filled bucket of string beans.

"I wonder what came this time?" she remarked, half running through the garden gate.

"*Ach*, Mandy, what's your hurry?" asked her sister.

Esther had been helping with the backbreaking task of picking beans.

"The better you stick to it, the sooner we'll be finished."

"I'll be back as soon as I get the mail," Mandy called over her shoulder. "I thought I saw him leave a package."

Now Esther remembered. Mandy had ordered a pair of shoes from the Sears catalog. Every day for a week, she kept expecting their arrival. Esther smiled to herself at Mandy's anticipation. *That girl is so impatient!* she thought.

Mandy took the mail to the house and then joined her sister once more.

"Well?" quizzed Esther.

"Well what?" Mandy remarked.

"*Sin sie kumme* (did they come)?"

"*Nee*, no," Mandy answered. "I can't understand why it takes so long."

"Well, anyway, you can still look forward to tomorrow's mail," Esther reminded her.

Mandy did not feel cheerful and wondered if her sister never experienced disappointment.

Finally, they reached the end of the last long row of beans. Straightening their aching backs and wiping the sweat from their faces, they carried the full pails to the house.

Kind mother that she was, Hannah told her daughters to rest a bit. She knew the girls were thirsty. As they washed their hands at the basin, she poured glasses of iced tea for them.

"By the way, Mandy, a letter came for you today. It was in with the other letters, and I guess you didn't see it. I put it on the sideboard."

"For me!" Mandy exclaimed in surprise.

"Ach, she was too busy looking for something big in the mail," Esther laughed. "She wanted shoes, not just a little old letter."

Nevertheless, Mandy quickly found the letter. Ignoring her sister's teasing, she fumbled to open it.

"Oh, who could it be from?" she wondered. "No one ever sent me a letter."

Without reading its contents, Mandy turned to the signature. "Why, it's from Lydia! I can't think why

117

she'd be writing to me."

"Want to know how you can find out?" Esther teased. "Read it!"

Mandy turned up her nose and marched off to read in privacy. She was not gone long.

Bursting into the kitchen and bubbling with excitement, she revealed the contents of the letter.

"Oh, Mom! It's from Lydia. She wants me to go to the singing next Sunday night. May I go? It would be my first time. She said we would sit together. Lydia has gone to singing four times already. She said she can tell me how to act. I'm sixteen now and ready for *Rumschpringe* (going with the young folks). May I, Mom?"

"If you stop long enough for me to get a word in edgewise, I'll answer," her mother responded. "You know your father and I will have to talk this over."

"But I can't wait," Mandy insisted.

"Well, you'll just have to wait. I'll bring it up with him tonight."

Mandy was thinking, *Can't Mother ever make any decisions on her own?* Mandy knew, however, that her chance of going was greater if she exercised patience, a virtue she sadly lacked.

Meanwhile, Mandy went about her work with a smile. She was looking forward to the joy of social life with her peers.

"Maybe my new shoes will come in time for me to wear them to the singing!" Mandy daydreamed.

"You don't know for sure if you can go," Esther reminded her. "Besides, are you going to sing, or to show off your shoes?"

"Both," Mandy saucily answered.

"Then maybe you shouldn't go!" Esther teased her.

"Oh, I think Mom and Dad will say 'yes.' "

"Wait and see."

"What are you girls talking about now?" asked their mother. She had come from the pantry and caught snatches of the lively conversation.

"Ach, Mandy is so *uff nemme* (taken up) with Lydia's letter. She thinks she's already at the youth singings."

"I do not," Mandy objected.

"It's so unusual for Mandy to get a letter. I can understand why she's so excited," Mom soothed them.

Mandy was grateful that Mother came to her defense.

"Well," Esther added, "for anyone who only seven months ago claimed she didn't think she cared to start Rumschpringe, you sure changed your mind."

"Oh, that was then, and this is now," Mandy replied. "Anyway, I was feeling so guilty about—" She couldn't finish the sentence. Were the old feelings of guilt returning to haunt her again? Mandy thought it had all been taken care of. Was she sure?

Esther looked at her sister. She wondered what she had said to upset Mandy. Sensing the change her remark brought on, Esther spoke more kindly. "Mandy, I'm glad Lydia invited you to join the youth. I really hope you can go Sunday night."

True to her word, Hannah Schrock did discuss the matter with her husband.

"What?" Lloyd exclaimed in mock surprise. "You mean to tell me our Mandy is old enough to go to the young folks singings! Well now, *ich wees net* (I don't know). *Was denkst du* (what do you think), Mom?"

"Well, she *is* sixteen. Esther would take her to the singings. It is all right with me if you agree."

Mandy was sitting behind the space heater, almost holding her breath as she waited for the answer.

"Mandy, do you think you're ready for this?" her dad asked. "Remember, you don't go only to have fun. We do want our youth to enjoy themselves, but you are also to be a Christian example. If you can do both, then you are ready."

"Oh, Dad, I know I can. I like being Amish and a Christian. I do enjoy that."

"You haven't been baptized and become a member of the *Gmee* (church) yet. But this doesn't mean you may do as you please. Remember what we've taught you and keep learning. When you go to hymn sing-ings, go for that purpose."

"Oh, Dad, you know I like to sing. Of course I'll help with the singing," Mandy replied.

"Naturally, we want you to fellowship with your friends there. I suppose it won't be long until some young whippersnapper will want to see you home." Her dad had a twinkle in his eye.

"Ach, Dad. I'll go with Esther. My friends, Alma, Erma, Lovina, Effie and Lydia have already started Rumschpringe. May I go, please?"

"We will try it and see how it goes," her Dad decided.

"Then I must answer Lydia right away. May I stay up later tonight to write a letter?"

"She'll see you when you get there," laughed

Mother. "But you so seldom get letters. Yes, if you don't stay up too long, you may answer her letter."

Mandy hurried for writing material and gladly wrote the message: "Lydia, I can come."

She would count the days, hours, and moments until Sunday. Just think, her first singing!

27
Mandy's First Singing

Church services had been at 'Stubble' Joe Marner's place. No one seemed to know why Joe was called by that name. They had moved into the community from Iowa, and the nickname came along and stuck to him. Now tonight the young people would gather at Joe's for the singing and fellowship.

"I'm glad you can go, Mandy," Esther told her sister. "Dad said we may drive Nell and go by ourselves, if we are careful. It will be nice that I don't need to ask the Byler young folks to take us along. We'll have fun driving together."

"Yes, we will," Mandy agreed. "We won't have far to drive tonight. Maybe that's why Dad is letting us go alone. I don't even care about the delay with the new shoes."

Both girls laughed. "I doubt anyone will even notice your shoes," Esther assured her.

Soon after chores and a light supper, the girls cooperated in hitching up Nell and then bid their parents good-bye.

"Be home by ten thirty," Lloyd Schrock instructed.

"I won't sleep till you're back," Hannah told them.

"*Ach*, Mom, don't worry. We'll be careful," Esther promised.

"Do you think I look all right?" Mandy asked as they drove along.

"Well, if you don't, it's too bad! I'm not turning around and going back. Of course you look all right. You are not thinking of impressing the *Buwe* (boys) so soon, are you?"

"*Sei net gegisch* (don't be silly)!" Mandy told Esther. "Weren't you nervous at your first singing?"

"Yes, I suppose I was, but you'll soon get used to it. By-and-by it'll be just like going to church."

"I hope I can sit with you and your friends," Mandy confided wistfully.

"You're a first-timer. We older girls sit on the girls' side of the table for more experienced singers, across from the older boys leading the singing. I thought you would want to be with Lydia, since she invited you."

"But what if Lydia can't come?" Mandy asked.

"If I know Lydia, she'll be there. She is one of the regulars. So are Alma and Erma. You'll find plenty of company."

Mandy's jitters were somewhat relieved when she saw Lydia waiting to meet her. As soon as Esther had tied Nell securely to a post, the two girls joined Lydia in the yard.

"*Ich bin froh* (I'm glad) you could come," Lydia told Mandy.

"Didn't you get my letter?" Mandy asked. "I wrote that I would."

"No, I didn't get a letter."

"Ach, that mail carrier is so slow," Mandy complained. "I sent for a pair of shoes several weeks ago. They haven't come yet!"

Esther and Lydia smiled at Mandy's frustration. It seemed comical that she blamed the mail carrier.

"Let's go in so we can find a good seat," Esther suggested.

Mandy and Lydia followed Esther, and soon Mandy was seated with Erma, Alma, and Lovina. Esther found a place with older girls at the singers' table.

The young folks visited for a while, but only until the first hymn was announced. Samuel Mast led the familiar German hymn "Das Loblied (The praise song)," always sung second at morning church services. They all joined in heartily.

One by one other German songs were chosen. These were all sung in unison. For forty-five minutes, the room rang with the old slow tunes. Then it was time for a break to rest their voices and enjoy cool, refreshing water.

During this break Mandy received another invitation from Lydia.

"Mandy," Lydia began, "do you remember telling me that Esther wants to take the winter off from *Maut* (hired girl) work? You said you might start working as a Maut then.

"Well, guess what! I'm hoping to start working at Laurel Valley Home, where they care for handicapped children. They really need more helpers. Wouldn't it be nice if we could work there together?"

This was a completely new idea for Mandy. She asked a few questions about the home and then responded, "I'd really like that. But what about transportation? It must be about ten miles to Laurel Valley. How would I get back and forth?"

"Here's the good part, Mandy. They send the groundskeeper in a van to pick up those who have no way. He would come for us on Monday morning and bring us home Friday after lunch. So we'd be home for weekends and wouldn't miss church services or singings."

"You mean you'd stay all week?" gasped Mandy.

"Yes. They furnish a nice room with two beds. We could room together. Our meals would be eaten with the residents.

"Best of all, our weekends would be free. The pay is better than housework, and I feel we would be helping those who really need it, who can't take care of themselves."

"Like Lloydie," remarked Mandy on impulse.

"Yes, some like Lloydie! But some children have other kinds of health problems, too."

Chills were going up and down Mandy's spine. Could God be giving her another chance? A chance to be kinder, more patient, and more loving toward a helpless soul?

"Think about it," Lydia urged. "We can talk about it some more."

Alma and Erma made it known that they would be interested also.

"Oh," exclaimed Mandy, "wouldn't that be nice if all of us could work there?"

"I know I can't," Lovina told the girls. "My mother needs me at home. There'll be another baby in October, so I'll be busy."

Mandy was shivering with excitement. She hardly noticed as the group became quieter and a song was chosen. Now they would sing some English hymns in four-part harmony, at a faster pace than the German hymns. How beautiful they sounded!

Mandy joined in the singing. When someone requested "Safe in the Arms of Jesus," tears filled her eyes. She knew that's where her dear little brother was, and it stirred her heart.

Time passed so quickly. Before Mandy thought it possible, Esther told her it was ten and they must start home. The singing part of the gathering was over, but some youths were still playing ring games in the yard. The Shrock sisters were among the first to leave.

Lydia's parting words to Mandy were about Laurel Valley Home: "Remember what I told you. Think it over, and let me know."

"What did Lydia mean by that remark?" Esther asked.

"I'll tell you on our way home," Mandy replied.

The girls had just turned onto the gravel road when something spooked Nell. The horse reared up on her hind legs. Next, she began to back up. Esther tried to steady her. Then a flash of light and a loud bang started Nell running at a fast pace.

"Whoa! Whoa!" Esther called.

But Nell kept running. The buggy swayed wildly.

Mandy clung to the seat with both hands. The dim buggy lights flickered so much that the girls feared they might go out completely.

"Can't you hold her back?" Mandy shouted.

"I'm trying!" Esther yelled back.

They were approaching the wide drive of the Mose Byler farm. Esther had an idea. If she could get Nell to turn into that drive and pull up to the barn, Nell might stop and calm down.

Esther pulled hard on the right rein, and the buggy bounced on two wheels into the lane. The girls were jolted all around. Mandy was hanging on and wondering if Esther knew what she was doing.

Sure enough, as the horse reached the barn, she stopped short. The sudden halt threw both girls from the seat onto the floor of the front buggy box.

Nell stood quivering and jumpy. It was hard to know who was frightened more—the girls or the horse. "*Wunderbaar* (wonderful)!" exclaimed Esther. "Are you all right, Mandy?"

"*Well, ich denk* (well, I think I am)."

They picked themselves up. Esther got out and gentled poor Nell. When the horse seemed quieted, Esther returned to the buggy.

"What a ride!" she commented. "It's a wonder Mose Byler didn't hear us and come to investigate."

"I'm surprised their dog didn't raise a fuss," Mandy replied.

"We probably scared him off, the way we came tearing in here."

Now that their fright had left them, the girls laughed about the wild ride.

"At the rate we drove, we'll be home well before ten thirty. Let's not mention this to the folks," Esther suggested. "They would just worry too much."

Mandy agreed. "There's no need to scare them too. But what do you think it was? What frightened Nell and made her take off like that?"

"I'm not sure, but I have an idea. It may have been some flashlight Simmies (show-offy boys) with firecrackers. It was a thoughtless trick since there could have been a bad accident.

"We must not forget to thank the Lord because I'm sure he was with us. Let's also remember to pray for whoever did such a deed."

Mandy did not forget to thank her heavenly Father for protection. Neither did she forget Lydia's invitation to work at Laurel Valley Home.

Her first singing—what an experience!

28
They Said Yes!

Mandy knew why her sister wanted a year off from *Maut* (hired-girl) duties. Esther had been keeping company with William Yoder for two years. Most of their visiting was by mail.

William lived in Indiana. Four or five times a year, he came to Ohio to visit his family. Esther frequently visited his family, especially when William was around.

Mandy was sure a wedding was in the making. Once her sister married, Mandy guessed that her own chances of being a Maut were slim. Her mother would need her help at home.

In recent years, her father was experiencing some health problems and would need her to help with the fieldwork. Her brother, Jonas, was a good worker, but the two could barely keep up with all that had to be done on the farm.

Therefore, Mandy decided to approach her parents

and propose that she become a Maut during the year Esther was home. If she got their okay on that, then she would bring up the opening at Laurel Valley Home.

Mandy had told Esther about Lydia's invitation for her to work at the Home. Her sister thought it was a good opportunity, but she wondered if the church and her parents would allow it.

"Mandy," Esther had said, *Du weescht es mir unser Leit helfe* (you know we help our own people). I've always worked for Amish families."

"But other people need help, too. Lydia told me they have children there with Down's syndrome, like Lloydie had. I'd like to help them."

"I hope you get to work there. It should not be as heavy work as helping other families. In my jobs as a Maut, I've done everything from housework to manure hauling. Really, Mandy, I hope you get this chance."

"*Danki* (thanks). So do I," Mandy answered.

The Schrock family was enjoying a relaxing Sunday at home. This was their in-between Sunday. That meant no services were held in their district.

They had neither been invited to Sunday dinner nor had they asked friends in. The day was spent in Bible reading, short naps, and sharing.

Several months had passed since Mandy started *rumschpringing* (going with the young folks). Whenever Lydia met her, she had the same question: "Did you ask your parents yet?"

Mandy would reply, "Not yet. I'm waiting for the right time."

Now is the time, Mandy decided on that quiet Sunday afternoon. Gathering up courage, she spoke with her parents.

"Mom, Dad, I want to ask you something." She hesitated.

"*Raus mit dann* (out with it, then)," her father invited.

"Now that Esther is staying home, may I be a Maut?"

"What? You aren't dry behind the ears yet," Lloyd teased.

Mandy saw the sly grin on her dad's face. He never passed up a chance for lighthearted fun.

"It's only fair," Hannah Schrock remarked. "The other girls all worked as Mauts."

"I can work hard, too," Mandy assured them.

"Oh, we know that," Lloyd admitted.

This was going to be easier than Mandy had thought it would be. But she hadn't reckoned with what their reaction might be after hearing all she had to propose.

"Who needs a Maut now?" her mother asked.

"I'm not thinking of housework."

"*Ya! Was dann* (yes! What then)?" Lloyd wondered.

"Lydia Yoder said they need girls to work at Laurel Valley Home. She's planning to start working there and—"

"Are you sure?" interrupted her father. "Did her parents say she could? And anyhow, I wonder if the bishop knows about this." Lloyd turned to his wife. "Do you think our church would allow it?"

"I don't know. It's never been done," Hannah replied.

Seeing the crestfallen look on her daughter's face, she continued, "It does seem like a nice Christian place. Once a month we older women go there to do mending. They're always so good to us. At mealtime, everyone prays together."

"That doesn't sound as worldly as some places, but it's sure not Amish," declared Dad.

"Why don't I talk with Lydia's mother?" Mom suggested. "You might ask the bishop, Lloyd, and find out how he feels about it."

A new thought entered Hannah's mind. "*Ach* (oh), but Mandy, how would you get to work each day?"

"That would be no problem," Mandy told them. "They send a van for us. Lydia said we would stay all week and come home on Friday. It would be almost like when you are a Maut for an Amish family.

"Lydia and I would share a bedroom. Oh, Mom, could I at least try it? Please? If it wouldn't work out, I could always come home."

"Give us some time to talk it over," her dad told her. "Are you sure you'd be satisfied with your Amish clothes, working among *die Weltleit* (the people of the world)? How soon might you want to go without your head cap?"

Mandy felt hurt that her Dad even thought of such things. "Ach, *Daed* (Dad)," she replied. "You know I wouldn't do any such thing."

"Right now you think you wouldn't, but temptation has changed many a person's mind. There would be *Englisch* (non-Amish) all around you, and maybe a few would even make fun of you."

"If some of the other girls worked there, we could

help one another be obedient," Mandy reasoned.

"*Du bist noch so yung* (you're still so young), but we hope we can trust you," commented Mother.

"Oh, you can! I know you can!" Mandy insisted.

"We certainly hope so," stated Dad.

"Then may I tell Lydia I can do it?"

"Now *waard* (wait)!" Lloyd demanded. "We haven't said yes—yet. Mother and I will talk it over some more, and I want to speak to the bishop.

"We don't want to do anything that's against the *Ordnung* (church rules). Since this is such a new thing, the church will help us decide what's right."

After services the following Sunday, Lydia asked Mandy once more. "Have you talked to your folks about you know what?"

"Of course I know what," Mandy strung her along.

"Well, what did they say? May you go?"

"They didn't say yes," Mandy told her dejectedly.

"But they didn't say no either, did they?" Lydia pressed.

"Not exactly."

"What do you mean—'not exactly'?"

"They want to think about it yet and talk to the bishop. My mom is going to ask your mom if she feels it's a good thing."

"My dad already talked with the bishop," Lydia told Mandy.

"Really? What did he say?"

"He said that as long as I stay within the rules of our church and dress Amish, he could permit it. But he didn't want me to be the only Amish girl working there. That's why I need you to come too."

"We aren't members of the church yet, Lydia."

"I know, but in a year I plan to be."

"So do I!" Mandy exclaimed. "Just think, Lydia. If we get to work together, we can make a lot of plans."

As the two girls made their way to the table for a bite to eat, they were joined by Alma, Erma, and Lovina.

"Where have you been?" asked Alma.

"We looked all over for you," Erma added.

"Out in the orchard, talking," Mandy told them.

"Talking about what?" wondered Erma.

"About working at Laurel Valley Home," Lydia answered.

"Oh, for sure. That's all you two think about anymore. Have your folks given their consent?"

"Mine have, but Mandy isn't sure yet."

"Look," Lovina pointed out, "there's your mother now, Mandy. She's asking Lydia's mother something. And . . . now your mother is smiling and nodding."

Mandy's heart seemed to skip a beat.

Lloyd also had a long talk with the bishop, who gave his consent to let the girls try, if they watched out for each other. But if they disobeyed the teachings of their parents or showed any signs of worldliness, it would be verboten (forbidden).

On the drive home, Mandy heard the words for which she had been waiting.

"Mandy, I spoke with the bishop today. He said as long as you obey what you've been taught, we may try letting you work at Laurel Valley."

Mandy could hardly contain herself, but she waited until her parents were finished.

"Whenever we women come to mend at the Home, I'll look in on you at work," promised her mom.

"Now don't let the *englisch* fashions there rub off on you," warned her dad. "Keep your plain dress and always wear the cap. And we'll count on you coming home every weekend, so you'll be with the family and won't need to miss church."

"Yes, Dad, I will! I will!"

Mandy felt like singing, crying for joy, laughing, even shouting. She would tell Lydia at the singing tonight. And she'd tell Alma, Erma, and Lovina, too. If any of them missed the singing, she would send them letters.

That night after the singing, she began writing to Alma, who had not come with the other young people. Her letter announced the good news: "Mom and Dad said yes!"

Little did she realize that within two months, six Amish girls would be employed at Laurel Valley Home, caring for handicapped children.

29
A Mysterious Way

Mandy loved her work at Laurel Valley Home. In fact, it didn't even seem like work. She had been there almost a year. Each person in her care was dear, but one was especially so.

Five-year-old Joey had captured her heart the day they met. He followed her everywhere. Joey was so like the brother she had lost!

"That boy is your shadow," Lydia told Mandy.

"Yes, it's hard to give attention as I should to my other friends. He gets so upset with me when I have to move on. But I can't make him understand that others have needs."

"What will he do when you leave? Your year is almost up, you know."

"Don't remind me," Mandy sighed. "I try not to think of that time. So many things are changing in my life."

The two girls had finished their day's work. As

they usually did, they hashed over the events of the previous weekend.

A soft knock sounded on their door. As Mandy opened it, the four other Amish girls entered.

"May we come in?" Alma asked.

Mandy laughed. "Looks like you're already in! Make yourself at home."

"I see they brought popcorn and orange drink, so let them stay!" Lydia quipped.

"You mean, if we came empty-handed, you would have kicked us out?" Erma pretended to pout.

"Not if you tell us who took you home from Sunday night's singing," Mandy teased.

"Oh, oh, Mandy," laughed Alma. "And who took *you* home?"

Mandy stuck her nose in the air, tilted her head, and remarked, "That's for me to know and you to find out." She busied herself clearing a place on the bedside stands to set out the glasses of orange drink and the dish of popcorn.

"Sit here on my bed," Lydia offered.

"You know we usually sit on the floor," Ada said. "Thanks anyway."

"Have we *verdutzt* (spoiled) anything by dropping in? What were you two going to do tonight?" Alma asked.

"No, you haven't verdutzt anything. Mandy was just telling me she feels so many things in her life are changing."

"If she keeps seeing Levi Slabach, I suppose there will be a change," Erma remarked.

"Be serious, won't you?" requested Mandy.

Almost apologetically, the laughing ceased.

"What things?" Alma asked. "Or don't you want to discuss it?"

"Oh, I don't mind. I feel the need to change and be baptized. Some of my motives have been selfish. My sister is to be married this fall. Oh, I wasn't to tell. Girls, please don't say I told!" Mandy insisted. "It was supposed to be a secret."

"We suspected it, but we won't tell," the girls assured her.

"I begrudged her that marriage because it means I must quit work here. Dad isn't well, and so they especially need help to keep the farm going.

"And I'll tell you something else if you promise to keep it. Yes, Levi Slabach has asked me to keep company with him. So there are changes and decisions. And, oh, what is best?"

"Didn't you say yes?" asked Ada.

"Yes what?" Mandy returned.

"Well, did you say yes to Levi?"

"*Ach,* Ada, you always were the *Bukeesich* (boy-crazy) type."

"I am not."

"No, I have not given Levi an answer yet. I'm not quite eighteen, and there's plenty of time," Mandy replied.

The evening passed pleasantly. After the girls played a few games of UNO, it was bedtime.

"Before you leave, why don't we have devotions together?" Mandy suggested.

She handed her Bible to Ada and let her choose a Scripture passage. Ada turned to Romans eight.

"I'll read from the beginning through verse twenty-eight. Tonight let's hear it in English. I understand it better that way."

The others agreed, so she began. Much of the reading told of the Spirit of God. This was Mandy's desire, to let the Spirit fill and lead her life. Then she would know that her choices were right.

The last verse Ada read was as follows:

"And we know that all things work together for good to them that love God, to them who are the called according to his purpose."

The girls knelt in silent meditation and prayer.

"Look what time it is," Erma remarked as their prayer ended. "We'd better get to bed."

Alma lingered a bit by the bedside stand as though reluctant to go.

"Come on, Alma, let's go," Erma urged her. Goodnights were said, and soon Mandy fell asleep.

The alarm clock startled her with its shrill clanging. Mandy wearily crawled from her bed and shut it off. She made her way to Lydia's bed and gently shook her awake.

"Come on, sleepyhead," Mandy yawned, "time to get up!"

"Already?" Lydia was rubbing her eyes.

"I'll get showered first," Mandy offered. "Maybe you can catch forty winks yet, but only forty."

She hurried through her morning routine. Fully dressed, she started to comb her hair while Lydia prepared for the day.

"Come on!" she called Lydia again.

"Alright, *ich bin wacker* (I'm awake)."

Mandy reflected upon last night's devotional reading and wondered what this day would hold for her. She would commit the day to the Lord. The promise from Romans was still fresh in her mind. Since she loved God, all things would work for her good.

That's it, she mused. *I don't have to worry at all about Dad's health, or the end of my work here at Laurel Valley. I don't have to be anxious about the answer I give Levi, or my decision about baptism. God knows my frustrations. He's well able to work them out for me, and with me.*

Lydia reentered the bedroom. Reaching for her cap on the bedside stand, she glanced at the alarm clock.

"Mandy," she exclaimed. *"Guck mol* (look once)! It's two o'clock in the morning!"

"Those girls," Mandy remarked. "I bet they had this planned. No wonder Alma wasn't in a hurry to leave. She was resetting our alarm!"

"Don't worry. We will get them back yet," Lydia vowed.

"Let's go back to bed," Mandy decided. "At least we can sleep a little later. We already had our showers and combed our hair. Let's act real spry and pretend nothing happened."

"Can you get back to sleep?" Lydia asked.

"I'm sure I can. My eyes are already closing." Mandy chuckled a bit as she climbed back into bed and settled down for the rest of her night's sleep.

Later in the day, the girls were waiting for the van to take them home for the weekend.

"Be sure to get plenty of sleep," Alma told Mandy and Lydia, "so you'll be able to *rumschpringe* (go to youth gatherings)."

140

"Oh, we will!"

All the Amish girls laughed so exuberantly that the receptionist wondered what was going on.

When Mandy reached home, she was surprised at the news awaiting her. Her parents were turning the farm over to her oldest sister, Susan, and her husband.

With their family and her brother, Jonas, still helping with farmwork, her dad could slow down. A vacant *Dawdyhaus* (grandparents' house) had been purchased and would be moved onto the homestead for her parents.

"Mom, this is all so sudden," Mandy commented. "Where will Jonas and I stay?"

"Ach, Mandy, Dad and I have been considering this for some time. Jonas and you will keep your rooms in the big house. Susan's girls will help me with my work.

"Since you've enjoyed your work at the home so much, you may keep on there if you want to. Dad and I are pleased you're content to keep our Amish ways. We think you're old enough to be *gedaaft* (baptized). What do you think?"

"Yes, Mom, I'm ready."

"We didn't know what we should do about the farm," Hannah Schrock said. "But last week it seemed that God worked it out for us. He works in strange ways."

"Always for our good," Mandy replied.

Hannah wondered at her daughter's remark, but she agreed.

At the Sunday-night singing, Mandy eagerly shared the good news with the girls close to her.

"I can stay on at Laurel Valley. And Mom thinks I'm old enough for baptism."

"We're happy for you," one of her friends told her.

"Yes, we sure are," echoed Lydia. "And I think I'll go into the instruction class with you to prepare for baptism, so we can *die Gmee nooch geh* (follow the church)."

"And now, are you going to make Levi happy, too?" Erma asked.

"Maybe. All I know is that 'God moves in a mysterious way, his wonders to perform,' as we sang in that one song tonight."

Mandy was happy. She thought of Joey and all the others in her care.

She glanced across the room and caught Levi's eyes, sparkling in return.

Mandy's cup overflowed.

The Author

Raised in the fertile farming community of Plain City, Ohio, Mary Christner Borntrager was seventh in an Amish family of ten children. In her series, Ellie's People, she depicts the Amish way of life in which she was raised.

At the age of nineteen, she married John Borntrager. They raised two boys and two girls.

Mary's education began with eight grades of elementary school. After leaving the Amish, she attended teacher-training institute at Eastern Mennonite College (now University), Harrisonburg, Virginia. For seven years she taught in a Christian day school. After she and her husband earned certificates in youth social work from the University of Wisconsin, they cared for emotionally disturbed and neglected youth.

Borntrager is a member of the Ohioana Library Association and the author of nine novels, listed on page 2. Page 6 shows a family tree of the fictional Ellie's People, with book titles in boldface type.

Because of reader interest, the author is kept busy with public speaking and autographing sessions. She has been interviewed on local TV and radio and receives many warm letters from her fans.

In 1994 Borntrager wrote a play based on her first novel, *Ellie*. It was presented to appreciative audiences at Hartville (Ohio) Mennonite Church, where she has been a member for forty years.

Mary's husband, John, passed away just before her first book was published. Now she is grandmother to eleven and great-grandmother to four children. She lives in North Canton, Ohio, with a granddaughter, who transcribed Borntrager's handwritten draft of this book into a word processor and printed it out.

Her hobbies include writing poetry, reading, quilting, memorizing the Bible, playing table games, and embroidering. She enjoys family reunions and get-togethers with her children and their families.

Borntrager is thankful for her Christian heritage and wants to pass it on. She hopes her series, Ellie's People, will bring pleasure to many readers and a better understanding of the Amish and their way of living.